FRENCH LEGENDS

TALES AND FAIRY

D0870621

Oxford Myths and Legends
in paperback

*

African Myths and Legends
Kathleen Arnott

English Fables and Fairy Stories
James Reeves

French Legends, Tales and Fairy Stories
Barbara Leonie Picard

Hungarian Folk-tales
Val Biro

Indian Tales and Legends
J E B Gray

Japanese Tales and Legends
Helen and William McAlpine

Russian Tales and Legends
Charles Downing

Scandinavian Legends and Folk-tales
Gwyn Jones

Scottish Folk-tales and Legends
Barbara Ker Wilson

West Indian Folk-tales
Philip Sherlock

The Iliad
Barbara Leonie Picard

The Odyssey
Barbara Leonie Picard

French Legends, Tales and Fairy Stories

Retold by
BARBARA LEONIE
PICARD

Illustrated by
JOAN
KIDDELL-MONROE

OXFORD UNIVERSITY PRESS
OXFORD   NEW YORK   TORONTO

Oxford University Press, Walton Street, Oxford OX2 6DP

Oxford New York Toronto
Delhi Bombay Calcutta Madras Karachi
Petaling Jaya Singapore Hong Kong Tokyo
Nairobi Dar es Salaam Cape Town
Melbourne Auckland

and associated companies in
Berlin Ibadan

Oxford is a trade mark of Oxford University Press

A CIP catalogue record for this book is available
from the British Library

ISBN 0 19 274149 7

Printed in Great Britain

Contents

TALES OF THE
FRENCH EPIC HEROES

Roland and Oliver

IN the days of the Emperor Charlemagne, Charles the Great of the Franks, who ruled France and Germany and fought so mightily against the enemies of Christendom, there lived a count named Girard. Count Girard held the city and the castle of Vienne and the land that lay about it, but he was no friend to his Emperor, and with his vassals and his knights he rebelled and made war on him. Charlemagne, much angered, called together his army and marched against Vienne, whilst Girard and his followers retreated into the city, defending the walls bravely. For many months the advantage fell to neither side, and time passed until the siege had lasted for two whole years, and many there were among the besiegers, as well as among the besieged, who longed for the war to be over. Yet the city could not be taken, so well was it defended, and Charlemagne, glad though he would have been to be at peace with all his subjects, could not bring himself to

3

withdraw his army, lest it should seem as though he acknowledged himself defeated by a rebel.

With the Emperor's army were those who were considered the great champions of France: Duke Naimes, his most trusted counsellor, Ganelon, who later brought such sorrow on France, Ogier the Dane, Yve and Yvoire, Gerin, Engelier the Gascon, Turpin the Archbishop of Rheims, who could wield a sword in defence of his faith as well as any knight, Duke Samson and brave Count Anseïs: ten champions famed throughout France.

There, too, with Charlemagne was his young nephew Roland, son of the Emperor's sister Berthe. Roland had but lately been knighted and he was anxious to prove himself, yet so long as the siege lasted it seemed as though he would have little chance of showing his worth. The days went slowly for him, and with the other young knights and the squires he often left the camp and hunted in the woods near Vienne, or jousted with his companions; and among them there was no one more skilled at feats of arms than he.

Count Girard also had a nephew, Oliver, of an age with Roland; and one day, for an adventure, carrying plain arms, that he might be unknown, Oliver slipped unseen through the gates of Vienne and wandered into the Emperor's camp. Here in an open space he found Roland and his companions tilting together, and after watching for a while, he asked if he might join them. Though he was a stranger to them, they thought him one of the Emperor's men, and they lent him a horse and let him tilt with them. Soon it was apparent that Oliver surpassed them all. Not even Roland, who was accounted the best among them, was more skilled with lance and sword.

The youths were loud in admiration of the stranger and asked his name, but he only smiled and would not answer. Then someone whispered that he might be an enemy, since in two years no one of them had seen him before. And the murmur went round amongst them, so that their friendly smiles were changed to suspicious frowns, and they crowded about him, demanding his name. Rough hands were laid upon him, but he broke free, and leaping on a horse, rode for his life towards the walls of Vienne.

'After him!' cried Roland. 'He must not escape. He is too good a prize to lose.' And the young knights rode after him swiftly with Roland at their head. Steadily Roland gained on Oliver, until he was upon him, and close beneath the city walls, Oliver turned to face his pursuers, and Roland, in triumph, raised his sword to strike. But at that moment there came a cry of terror from the walls above, and Roland looked up and saw a maiden, the fairest he had ever seen, standing on the ramparts, her hands clasped in supplication and her face pale with fear. It was lovely Aude, the sister of Oliver. 'Spare my brother Oliver,' she pleaded. And Roland, staring at her, slowly lowered his sword and let Oliver ride on to the gates unharmed. 'I could not bring grief to so fair a maiden,' he said to himself.

During the days that followed, Roland thought much on Oliver and Aude, and wished that they had not been the Emperor's enemies. And for their part, they thought of Roland, and wished the war were at an end; and Oliver sought to persuade his uncle to peace.

After a time, his nephew's counsels prevailed, and Count Girard sent Oliver, well attended, to Charlemagne to ask that they might be accorded. 'If you will withdraw your army, sire, my uncle the Count will come forth from Vienne and swear allegiance, and he will serve you faithfully for all his life,' said Oliver.

But the Emperor, for all that he hated warring against his own vassals, could not find it in his heart to forgive Girard his rebellion so easily. 'Let Count Girard humble himself before me, and I will consider pardoning him,' he said.

'Sire,' replied Oliver, 'that would my uncle never do.'

'Then the war goes on,' said Charlemagne. But Duke Naimes spoke to him, counselling peace.

Oliver, standing before the Emperor, turned his head and looked at Roland and saw how he was watching him. He smiled and said impulsively, 'You and I are of an age and well matched. How say you, if our uncles are willing, shall we settle this war in single combat?'

'Gladly,' said Roland, and he begged the Emperor's permission. After thought, Charlemagne agreed. 'Go back and tell Count Girard,' he said to Oliver, 'that if you are victorious in this contest I will depart from his lands with all my army, and leave him in peace for ever. But if my nephew Roland is the victor, then must Count Girard lose Vienne and all his lands to me.'

'I shall tell him,' said Oliver; and he returned to the city.

And so it was decided that the outcome of the war should be determined by single combat between the two young knights, and a day was named upon which they should meet on a little isle in a river that ran between the camp and the city walls.

On the appointed day, Roland, armed and carrying his sword Durendal, which no blade could withstand, went to the islet to await Oliver. Soon Count Girard's nephew came out through the city gates, wearing the armour and bearing the sword which had been given to him by a good Jew of Vienne on the day he had been made a knight.

Eagerly all those from the Emperor's camp crowded about Charlemagne and the champions of France upon the bank of the river to watch the fight, whilst Count Girard and his family, and Aude with them, stood upon the walls of Vienne with the defenders of the city.

The two young men greeted each other courteously, and at once the battle began. They were indeed well matched, giving blow for blow; and at any one of their strokes a lesser knight would have fallen. Soon their shields were dented and their armour battered, links from their chain mail falling about them as they hacked with their good swords. But at last with a great stroke from Durendal, the strongest sword in all France, Oliver's blade was broken and he fell to his knees with the force of the blow. A cry of fear went up from the watchers on the walls of Vienne, but from the Emperor's knights a shout of triumph rose. Oliver thought, 'My last moment is come,' and he braced himself to meet the stroke which would end his life. But Roland flung Durendal aside. 'I cannot slay an unarmed man,' he said.

Oliver rose, and he and Roland tore up two saplings to

7

serve them as clubs, and with these they continued their fight until the green wood was broken all to splinters. And then the young knights wrestled together, each striving unsuccessfully to throw the other, until, at midday, both locked in each other's grip, they fell to the ground at the same time, so that neither could be said to have thrown the other. They stood up, breathless and exhausted. 'The sun is high,' said Roland. 'It is too hot for fighting. Let us rest awhile.'

They took off their helmets and smiled at one another. 'I am happy,' said Oliver, 'that I am privileged to fight with so worthy an enemy.' And the two young men embraced and sat down upon the grass and talked together as though they had been old friends. Wine was brought to them from the city, and another sword for Oliver; and when an hour or two had passed and the sun was lower in the sky, they helped each other to arm again, and once more began their fight.

As before, neither proved the better, and for long the battle raged, until suddenly, stepping aside to avoid a blow from Oliver, Roland lowered his sword and said, 'Stay your hand awhile, for I feel a weakness come over me as though I had a fever, and I would rest.'

With courtesy Oliver set aside his sword. 'Rest for as long as you need, good Roland. I would not wish to be victor because you are unwell. Lie down and I will watch over you.'

Roland, who was merely feigning sickness in order to test Oliver, took off his helmet and lay down upon the grass. Oliver placed his shield beneath his head to serve him as a pillow and fetched water for him from the river in his own helmet.

Watching, Charlemagne thought, 'My nephew is vanquished and I have lost the day.' While from the walls of Vienne fair Aude watched with pity; for though her brother's cause was hers, from her first sight of him she had felt a great admiration for Roland, an admiration which she knew could very easily turn to love.

But Roland sprang to his feet and laughed. 'I did but try you, Oliver. And so courteously have you treated me that I wish we were brothers or friends, and not enemies.'

'Brothers we could be,' replied Oliver. 'If we both live through this battle, I will give you my sister for your wife, since there is no other to whom I would rather see her wed. And as for friends, are we not friends already in our hearts?'

They fell once more to fighting, and again the advantage lay with neither, and still they fought as the sun went down the sky and sank from sight. Through the twilight they fought, while the watchers strained their eyes to see them and could not tell one from the other; and on into the darkness, so that only the sound of metal clashing upon metal told that the battle still went on.

And then at last from the darkness there was silence, as with one accord they ceased their strife. 'Heaven does not mean that to either of us shall be the victory,' they said. And they threw down their weapons and embraced, swearing friendship for ever. 'Never again shall we take arms against each other,' they vowed.

Each of them persuaded his uncle to be at peace, and for love of them Charlemagne and Count Girard were

9

accorded, uniting against their common enemies, the Saracens, who held all Spain and were attacking France. And on a happy May morning Roland and Aude were betrothed, to their great joy and Oliver's.

From the day of their battle Roland and Oliver were comrades in arms, riding together against the Saracens and fighting side by side, winning such fame that they were accounted amongst the champions of France, the foremost of the twelve. Roland was ever brave, brave to the point of rashness, and very proud, and he hated the Saracens with all his heart and never trusted them. But Oliver, though no less brave, was gentle and cautious and never set his own glory before the good of France. Many adventures did the two young knights have in the years they were together, and until the day they died they were never parted.

The Battle at Roncevalles

WITH his twelve champions the Emperor Charlemagne fought for seven years against the Saracens in Spain, and at the end of that time all the land had yielded to him save only Saragossa which a certain King Marsile still held. Marsile awaited aid from his overlord, the Emperor Baligant, who ruled the eastern world, and to gain time he sent cunningly to Charlemagne with offers of friendship. Charlemagne was at Cordova when Marsile's messengers came to him, bearing olive branches in token of peace. 'We bring you word from our king,' they said. 'He promises that if you will withdraw your army out of Spain, he will give up his old faith and be baptized a Christian, and take you for his liege lord and hold his lands from you. He will, moreover, give you great store of gold and precious gems.'

Charlemagne thought long on this offer, and then he

called to council his twelve champions and told them of it. 'What is your advice, my lords?' he asked.

Hardly had he finished speaking before his nephew Roland stepped forward. 'Do not trust Marsile, sire, for once before he gave us fair words and a greeting, yet when you sent two knights to bear your answer to him, treacherously he slew them. Let us instead lay siege to Saragossa and slay Marsile and all his men.'

When young Roland had ceased, Ganelon, who had married his widowed mother, stood up. 'There spoke one who thinks more of his own battle glory than of God's honour. My stepson is rash and boastful; do not listen to him, sire. Surely it would be a greater triumph for Christendom if Marsile were to be baptized than if he were to be slain? My counsel is that you accept his offer, sire.'

'Indeed, Count Ganelon has spoken wisely,' said old Duke Naimes, to whose words the Emperor always listened, 'and we should do well to heed him.'

After he had considered for a time, Charlemagne said, 'I will accept King Marsile's offer, and a messenger shall go to him to tell him of it. Now, whom out of all my knights shall I send to Saragossa?'

But at his words everyone was silent, remembering the fate of the last two messengers their Emperor had sent to King Marsile. Then Roland said scornfully, 'I would be glad enough to go.'

'Not you, Roland, of all men,' said Oliver, 'for you would speak proud words to King Marsile and anger him, and ruin all. It would be better I went myself.'

'It shall be neither you, Oliver, nor yet my nephew

Roland,' said Charlemagne. 'It shall be an older man. Come, my lords, chose me out one of your number to bear my answer to King Marsile.'

Yet still were they all silent, fearing treachery, and they would not name one of their company, lest harm should come to him. Then Roland laughed, 'Send Ganelon my stepfather, sire, since it is he who counsels you to trust Marsile.'

The Emperor did not choose to see his nephew's irony. 'That is well spoken,' he said. 'Ganelon is wise and his words are ever prudent. Ganelon shall bear my answer to Marsile.'

With amusement, Roland watched the anger of the stepfather whom he had never liked, as Ganelon turned to him, his blue eyes hard with hatred. 'No doubt it would please you well should I never return from Saragossa. But I promise you, Roland, if God is good to me, and I return safely, you shall repent it.'

But Roland only laughed and turned his back and spoke with Oliver.

So Count Ganelon rode to Saragossa to King Marsile, and all along the way he thought with hatred of Roland, and considered how he might be rid of him. Marsile received him graciously and bade him speak. 'Lord king,' said Ganelon, 'my most noble Emperor accepts your offer. But if you fail to keep your word, he will lay siege to Saragossa and burn it utterly. All your men will he slay, and you yourself will he carry into France to die a shameful death. Thus has he bidden me say to you.'

Marsile was angered at these words, and he took up his spear and would have struck down Ganelon, but that his nobles held him back. After a time he grew calm, thinking how he must delay until Baligant could come, and he spoke quietly. 'What I have offered I will fulfil. Now tell me, good Count Ganelon, about your Emperor Charles.'

'What shall I tell you of him, save that he is the mightiest man in all the world?' said Ganelon with pride.

'Mighty he may be,' replied Marsile, 'yet he is old, and were I to fight against him with all my men, I should easily overcome him, the greybeard.'

'You would be defeated utterly,' said Ganelon in scorn. And then it came into his mind how he might do harm to Roland, and yet be loyal to Charlemagne. He smiled a little. 'But perhaps you are right, lord king. He is indeed growing old, and he relies much on his nephew Count Roland. Well would it be for you and for all the Saracens were Roland slain, for then would the Emperor have lost his right hand.'

King Marsile looked long at Ganelon, and then he said, 'Good Count Ganelon, how may Roland be slain?'

Ganelon leant forward and spoke quietly. 'When the Emperor withdraws his army into France, he will, as is his custom, leave behind him a rearguard to cover his retreat. It could be contrived that Count Roland would lead this rearguard. When the Emperor is well on his way, come with your men and fall upon the rearguard in the Pass of Roncevalles. Thus may you slay Roland.'

Marsile smiled. 'It is good counsel you have given me, and I will reward you well for it.' But Ganelon cared nothing for gold or silver or jewels, he longed only that Roland might be dead.

'Will you give me your oath that Roland will be with the rearguard?' asked Marsile; and Ganelon swore it upon his sword. And so was the treachery agreed upon, and Ganelon rode back to Cordova with word to the Emperor from King Marsile, of his friendship and his desire for baptism.

'It is well,' said Charlemagne. 'Let us prepare to return to France. But first, my lords, who shall lead the rearguard to cover our withdrawal?'

Ganelon said quickly, 'Let it be my stepson Roland, sire. For he is brave, as we all know.'

'It shall be my dear nephew Roland,' agreed the Emperor.

But Roland turned to Ganelon. 'No doubt you hope that some danger may threaten the rearguard that you offer my name as its leader. Yet for all that, sir stepfather, I thank you, that you have given me yet another chance to show my valour. For I swear that with me to guard his withdrawal, our Emperor shall lose not even a single pack-horse.'

Ganelon smiled. 'It was for that reason I named you, Roland, and not in any hope of danger.'

Oliver came and stood beside his friend. 'I will remain in the rearguard with you, Roland.' And after him came others of the champions of France: Gerin, Yve and Yvoire, Engelier, Anseïs and Samson, all to take their place with Roland as their leader. Archbishop Turpin of Rheims, as good a warrior as any knight, seeing them, said, 'By my faith, I will join with you too, good Roland.'

Then, when Roland and the others had chosen out

15

twenty thousand men, and Ogier the Dane had been sent forward with a vanguard to prepare the Emperor's way, Charlemagne mounted his great war-horse, and with Duke Naimes at one side of him and Ganelon at the other, he rode away for France at the head of his huge army, through the Pass of Roncevalles and on towards the borders of Gascony.

When the army and the Emperor had been long out of sight, there came a mighty sound of trumpets from beyond the hills to the south. 'It is the Saracens,' said Oliver. 'God forbid that King Marsile has broken his word and comes to take us by surprise.'

'What of it if he has?' said Roland. 'I should not be sorry to fight once more for my uncle's sake. A true knight should ever be ready to suffer in his liege lord's cause. If it should come to battle, let all men here take me for an example.'

But Oliver climbed upon a high rock and looked down into the valley before him; and there he saw the great army of the Saracens, one hundred thousand strong, all bound for the Pass of Roncevalles. The sun shone on their lances and on their helmets and on the gay colours of their cloaks and the pennons flying in the breeze. 'God have mercy on us, for we are quite outnumbered,' thought Oliver. He went down the hill to Roland and told him of what he had seen. 'It must be that Count Ganelon betrayed us to Marsile,' he said.

'Ganelon is my mother's husband. I will permit no word against him,' said Roland.

'Take your horn, Roland, and blow a loud blast upon it,

16

and our lord the Emperor will hear and know we are in danger, and he will return with all his men.'

Roland looked at Oliver with scorn. 'Would you have me lose the fame I have in France? Would you have me proclaim myself a coward who cries for help? No, I have Durendal, my good sword, with me, and I shall account for many unbelievers' lives today.'

'Roland, dear friend,' pleaded Oliver, 'blow your horn, or we shall never see France again.'

'God forbid that it should ever be said of me that I blew my horn for fear of any man.'

'Where is the shame,' asked Oliver, 'when they are five to our one?'

Roland's head was high in pride. 'I would rather die than be so dishonoured.' And Oliver knew that it was useless to speak further.

The Franks made ready for battle, and Archbishop Turpin rode to the top of a little hill and spoke to them, bidding them fight bravely. 'Fight,' he said, 'for the glory of God against these unbelievers, and if you should be slain, why, your souls will be welcomed in paradise.' Then every man knelt down, and Turpin blessed them all.

When each knight was armed and mounted on his horse, Roland led the Franks through the pass and on to the plain where the Saracen host was spread. He drew his sword Durendal and raised it high. 'Let us fight,' he cried, 'for God and for France and for our Emperor Charlemagne.' And from the ranks of the men of France went up the battle cry of Charlemagne: 'Montjoy!' And they spurred on their horses and rode against the great army of Marsile.

Many were the Saracen lords who fell in that first charge, and many more fell after to the swords and lances of the Franks; and bravely did Roland and Oliver and the other champions of France acquit themselves. Oliver fought so mightily with his lance that he had no time to draw Hautclere his sword; but when his lance was shattered, then Hautclere flashed in the sun, and at each stroke a Saracen warrior was cut down by its keen blade. As though he had been no priest, Archbishop Turpin struck a hundred blows, crying out on unbelievers until they fled from him.

But at last, for all the courage of the Franks, the greater numbers prevailed, as they were bound to do, and one by one the Emperor's noble champions fell dead: Duke Samson, Engelier from Gascony, Count Anseïs, Gerin, Yve and

Yvoire; until only Roland and Oliver and the Archbishop remained. Then Roland spoke to Oliver. 'The noblest men of the Franks are dead, the land of France will miss them sorely. I would that my uncle were here.' He took his ivory horn from where it hung about his neck. 'I shall sound my horn, Oliver, that he may come to our aid.'

Oliver stared at him amazed. 'You would not sound your horn when I pleaded with you. Will you sound it now? You would not sound your horn when it would have saved the lives of our good comrades who lie dead. Will you sound it now to save yourself? Never will I permit it.' With scorn he gave back to Roland his own words, 'I would rather die than be so dishonoured.'

'Oliver, dear friend, why are you so angered with me?' asked Roland.

'Because foolhardiness is not courage. Today, by your boastfulness and pride, you have lost our lord the Emperor the finest men in France. Had you sounded your horn when I counselled it, the Emperor would be with us now, and King Marsile would be slain or a prisoner. You are the bravest and noblest of all knights, Roland, and never shall the world see your like. But after today, when the Emperor Charlemagne has need of you, he will seek you in vain, for you will not be there to serve him. And this day also, must our great friendship come to an end in death.'

Hearing them, Turpin came to them. 'Count Roland and Count Oliver, this is no time to quarrel. Small good will it do us if the horn is sounded now, for we shall be slain before the Emperor can reach us. Yet it were best to sound it, that he may return and avenge us all, as he would wish to do.'

So Roland blew a blast upon his ivory horn, and thirty leagues away, Charlemagne heard it and said, 'That is Roland's horn. Our men are in battle.' But Ganelon said, 'That cannot be, sire.'

A second time Roland sounded his horn, and Charlemagne heard it and said, 'That is Roland's horn. He is in danger, or he would not sound it.' But Ganelon laughed and said, 'No doubt Roland hunts and would tell his men that he has killed his quarry. Roland was ever boastful, he would blow his horn all day for but a single hare. Let us ride on, sire, for we are yet far from France.'

A third time Roland sounded his horn, with all the strength he had, and Charlemagne heard it. 'That was a long blast,' he said, and reined in his horse.

'Whoever blew that horn is in mortal danger,' said Duke Naimes. 'Someone has betrayed us.' And Charlemagne turned and looked long at Ganelon. Then he gave orders for the trumpets to be sounded and for all knights to ride with him back to the Pass of Roncevalles. But Ganelon he handed over to his scullions as a prisoner, with orders that they were to guard him well.

In the pass, Roland hung his horn once more about his neck. 'Oliver, my friend, and you, good Archbishop, let us fight while life remains to us.' And he rode yet again into the battle and sought out King Marsile. King Marsile's son he slew with one mighty stroke, and with another he struck off Marsile's right hand, so that the Saracen king fled, and many of his men with him. But there were yet thousands left.

Oliver was sorely wounded by a Saracen nobleman, and knew he had not long to live. But with all his might he returned the blow, so that his assailant fell dead. 'Now can you never boast at home how you slew Oliver,' he said. He went about the plain, striking blow after blow, but so weak was he from loss of blood, that his sight grew dim and he did not know friend from foe; and in this way, coming upon Roland, he struck at his friend. Remembering their quarrel, Roland said gently, 'It is I, Roland, your friend who loves you. You did not challenge me. Did you mean that blow?'

Oliver swayed in his saddle as though he would have fallen. 'Forgive me, dear friend. I cannot see, though I can hear your voice.'

'You did not hurt me,' said Roland, 'there is nothing to forgive.' And there upon the battlefield, for the last time, they embraced. And Oliver dismounted from his horse and fell to the ground and died. Roland wept for him. 'Oliver, my friend,' he said, 'we have been comrades for many years, and now you lie dead while I still live.'

By then all the Franks were slain, save only Roland and Turpin, and Turpin's horse had been killed so that he had to fight on foot, and beneath a great press of javelins and arrows he fell. Roland's horse also, the Saracens slew; and then they fled, to join their king, Marsile.

Roland went to Turpin and bound up his wounds. Then he fetched from where they lay, the bodies of the slain champions of France: Yve and Yvoire, Engelier from

Gascony, Gerin, Anseïs and Duke Samson, and laid them before Turpin. 'Bless our comrades, lord Archbishop,' he said. And Turpin sat up upon the ground and blessed the dead knights and absolved them from their sins. Then lastly Roland fetched Oliver and laid him on his shield, kneeling beside him, weeping, while Turpin blessed him also. 'Oh, Oliver, my friend,' whispered Roland, 'in no land in all the world was there a better knight.' And in his grief and the pain of his wounds, he fell senseless. Seeing him, Turpin rose and took the horn from about his neck, thinking to fetch him water from a stream that ran near by, but he was too weak to walk even a little distance, and he fell forward and died.

When Roland recovered his senses, he saw how Turpin, too, was dead, and going to him, he laid him on his back and crossed his hands upon his breast. 'God welcome you in paradise, brave Archbishop,' he said.

Then he took up his horn from where it had fallen, and holding Durendal his sword, he went slowly across a trampled cornfield towards a little hill. At the top of the hill he sat down upon the grass. A Saracen who had all this time been watching him, feigning to be dead, crept close, that he might steal his sword. But Roland saw him come, and struck him upon the head with his horn, with such force that the man was slain and the horn was broken.

After a little time, Roland looked at his sword. 'My good Durendal, I have done great deeds with you. By your help, many lands have I conquered for my uncle; but now I have no more need of you. Yet never shall any other man call you his own.' He rose, and going to a rock close by, he raised the sword to shatter it upon the hard stone, but the steel held and did not break. Again he struck, and the rock was broken, but the good sword was still whole. When he saw that he might not break Durendal, Roland set it on the grass, and beside it, his horn of ivory; then he laid himself upon them that the Saracens might not find them. With his face towards Spain, that Charlemagne might see how he had died undefeated, he prayed God's forgiveness for his sins, and so died.

When the Emperor came to Roncevalles, he found all his rearguard dead; but with his army he pursued the Saracens even to the walls of Saragossa, slaying them by thousands. Then he saw buried with reverence all his knights who had fallen in the pass, and he mourned unceasingly for Roland, his nephew. 'Who will now fight for me,' he said, 'since Roland is dead? Who will now honour me, since Roland is dead? I have no more wish to live, since Roland, my nephew, is dead.' And he wept.

But Charlemagne lived to avenge the deaths of his champions, in a great battle against Baligant, the emperor from the east, whom he slew in single combat. When King Marsile heard word of the death of his overlord, he died from grief, and Saragossa fell to the Franks.

His task of vengeance in Spain accomplished, the Emperor returned to France; and there Ganelon was judged and sentenced and put to death, and so were Roland and Oliver and the dead champions of France fully avenged.

Guillaume of Orange

AFTER the battle of Roncevalles, during the last years
of the reign of Charlemagne, a good knight named
Guillaume fought bravely for his emperor against
the Saracens. He was an honest, outspoken man, with a
great devotion to his family: his parents and his brothers
and their children. He was a fine judge of horses, and best
of all the spoils he took from the Saracens he accounted
their swift steeds. But always his favourite horse was his
own piebald Baucent, to whom he would speak as though
it had been a person, and in reply it would neigh or
shake its head or paw the ground as if it had understood
him.

When Charlemagne died, he was succeeded by his weak
and foolish son, Louis. Louis was such a man as the hardy
Guillaume would have despised, but because he was his
Emperor, Guillaume served him faithfully and was ever
loyal to him. Guillaume had a sister, Blanchefleur, and for
her beauty, Louis married her, and she spoke much in the

interests of her brothers at the Emperor's court, so that Louis might listen and favour them.

Many were the adventures Guillaume had against the Saracens. Once he saved the life of the cowardly Emperor Louis as he fled from his enemies. And once in single combat with a huge warrior named Corsolt, a great champion of the Saracens, as tall and broad as a giant, he received a sword stroke which cut off the end of his nose, so that ever after he was called Guillaume Shortnose, and many were the jests made at his expense. But he killed Corsolt and so avenged the blow, and to the jests he only said, 'What of it? The shortening of my nose will have lengthened my good fame, I have no doubt.'

One day he reminded the Emperor Louis of how he had fought long for his sake. 'Yet little have you rewarded me, sire,' he said. 'Give me, I pray, lands that I may call my own.'

And after he had considered, Louis answered, 'I give to you the towns of Nîmes and Orange. Thus shall I reward you.'

Now, Nîmes and Orange, in the south of France, had long been in the hands of the Saracens, so they were a poor reward, but Guillaume was undaunted. He called together his followers and his kinsmen, and they marched first against Nîmes. 'The town is well defended,' said his men, 'how is it possible that we shall take it?'

'I shall find a way,' replied Guillaume confidently.

On the road to Nîmes they passed a peasant driving an ox which pulled a simple cart made of a barrel upon wheels. This cart was filled with salt which the peasant hoped to sell in the town, and upon the top of the salt sat the peasant's children, laughing and playing at marbles. Guillaume stared at this peaceable sight, and then he gave a great laugh. 'Let us make ourselves carts,' he said, 'and in the guise of merchants enter Nîmes. Thus shall we take the town.' In spite of the protests of his knights, who, garbed as poor merchants, had to help drag the frail carts along the rough road, heaving the wheels out of ruts and over stones, it was done; and so, by Guillaume's cunning, the town of Nîmes was taken.

'Next falls Orange,' said Guillaume, well pleased with himself. Orange was in the power of the Saracen Emir Tiebaut, and was well guarded from attack, so Guillaume entered the town alone, disguised as a Saracen, to spy out the defences. But he was discovered and captured, and cast into prison; and the Emir Tiebaut, being about to journey from the town for a few days, left Guillaume in the charge of his wife, Orable, bidding her guard him well; for he wished, on his return, to offer Guillaume his life if he would renounce the Christian faith. Orable was curious to see the brave Frankish knight who had come alone into Orange, so she went herself to the dungeon where he lay to look at him. Though Guillaume was no longer young, and, lacking the end of his nose, he was far from handsome, his courage and his bearing won both her respect and her heart, and she promised to help him escape. But Guillaume's kinsmen and knights came with an army to rescue him; and when the Emir Tiebaut returned there was a great battle at Orange in which he was killed, and so the Saracens fled from the town. Thus did Guillaume win for himself both Nîmes and Orange, which Louis had given him.

As for Orable, she received Christianity and was baptized in the name of Guibourg, and Guillaume married her; and a more loyal wife few men could have had. But Blanchefleur was jealous of her beauty, and ceased to use her influence with the Emperor in her brother's favour, so that Louis was even more grudging than before with praise and gifts to Guillaume.

Guillaume and Guibourg had no children of their own, but they adopted two of Guillaume's nephews, Vivien and his little brother Gui. Vivien was a brave youth who longed to win great fame for himself. On the day that he was knighted by his uncle he swore an oath. 'Never shall I retreat one step before the Saracens or any enemies of France,' he vowed.

'A short life have you promised yourself, and much mourning for your kinsmen,' said Guillaume dryly, when he heard of it.

Soon after, the Saracens invaded Aquitaine in their thousands, and though the Emperor Louis sent little help, Guillaume and Vivien and their men fought bravely against them on the plain of Aliscans. Vivien proved himself a valiant knight, fearing no man, and giving and taking fierce blows. But once, while the battle raged, as he charged at a band of warriors from Africa and saw their black, wild faces, he thought, 'Surely they must be fiends come from hell,' and he held his horse and drew back the length of a lance. Then, ashamed, he rode on, hewing left and right with his sword, and the black heads rolled about him, and the savage warriors fell to the ground.

Yet for all the courage of the Franks, they were outnumbered, and without the help of the Emperor, they could not hope to prevail. And Guillaume, most of his men dead, searching on the battlefield for Vivien, found him dying. He dismounted and knelt beside him and took him in his arms. 'Alas,' he said, 'he was a lion in courage, a great terror to the Saracens, yet gentle to his friends, my good nephew Vivien. I shall not see his like again.'

Vivien opened his eyes and stirred a little. 'Good uncle, I am dying, and I have a great sin upon my conscience, but there is no priest here to absolve me.'

'Tell me the sin, since there is no priest, and God will understand,' said Guillaume.

'Good uncle, on the day that you made me a knight, I swore that never should I retreat before my enemies. Yet today I broke that oath.' And he told how he had given way before the savage warriors, thinking them to be fiends. 'Uncle, it was a great sin, and bitterly do I repent it.'

'Have no fear,' said Guillaume gently, 'for God will pardon it.'

Comforted, Vivien smiled. He spoke once more before he died. 'Good uncle, carry my last greeting back to my aunt Guibourg, for she loved me as if I had been her own son.'

When Vivien was dead, Guillaume escaped from the battlefield wearing the armour and the clothes of a dead Saracen, and thus he was able to reach Orange safely, with news of the defeat of the Franks. Together he and Guibourg wept for the death of Vivien. At last she dried her tears. 'He must be avenged,' she said. But Guillaume had no heart for further fighting. 'And besides,' he said, 'what hope have we without the Emperor's aid?'

'It would have been better had you died on the plain of Aliscans than that you should bring shame on your family by giving up the fight,' said Guibourg. And then she told him how, while he was in battle, she had called to Orange as many knights as would come. 'They are no great army, but they are here in the castle. Take them and ride back to Aliscans.'

'Do you expect them to ride out to certain death?' asked Guillaume bitterly.

'With your permission, lord, I shall go to them now, and I shall not tell them the truth. I shall rather say that on the battlefield great spoils await them, arms and armour and horses from the fleeing Saracens. They shall not know that the enemy won the day.'

'As you will,' said Guillaume wearily.

Guibourg, with a smile and humming a gay air, went to where the knights waited, and with a feigned joyfulness she was far from feeling, she told them of the booty that was lying on the plain. And they one and all agreed eagerly to ride with Guillaume to the battlefield. Then Guibourg set food and drink before her lord: a large loaf, a shoulder of boar, a roasted peacock, a brawn of pork, two big cakes to finish the meal, and a huge goblet of wine. And Guillaume, who had thought he could never care for food again, ate every morsel, while Guibourg watched him. Then she laughed, though shakily, and said, 'The man who

29

could eat so large a meal must surely be a strong and dangerous enemy.'

After he had eaten, Guillaume prepared to go once more to fight. 'Take good care of little Gui,' he said. 'Do not let him out of your sight, for he is all that is left to us, now that Vivien is dead.' And this Guibourg promised to do. Then Guillaume, with the knights his lady had called together, rode from the castle of Orange, and Guibourg and young Gui watched him, waving their farewells and calling for God's blessing on him. But when Guillaume was out of sight, the boy began to weep. When Guibourg sought to comfort him, he said, 'Why should my lord uncle consider me a child? I am no coward, and I would go to fight at his side.'

'It is his wish, and mine, that you remain here with me,' said Guibourg.

But Gui only wept the more. 'My uncle will not have one kinsman with him when he next draws his sword against the enemy. Let me go with him, good aunt.'

'Your uncle will be angry if I do not obey him and keep you safely here. You would not wish that, would you, my nephew?'

Gui dried his tears and looked at her. 'I can lie to him, good aunt, and say I ran away from you.' He caught at her hand, coaxingly. 'Let me ride after him. I promise I will care for him well and bring him safely home to you.'

And Guibourg had not the heart to deny him, and she gave him her own horse. With a saddle that was too large for him, and with the stirrups shortened to fit his little legs,

Gui rode off happily and joined the squires who followed
Guillaume's knights.

Some distance from Orange, Guillaume paused to speak
to his men and offer them encouragement, for well he remembered that they had followed him for spoils and not

for fighting. Proudly he surveyed them drawn up before
him. 'No one, my friends, I dare swear, save the Emperor
Louis himself, could call upon so fine an army. We should
do great things against our enemies and the enemies of
France. And not only from the knights do I hope for courage and feats of arms, but from their squires as well.' He
looked past the knights to where the squires waited a short
way off. Then he caught sight of little Gui on his big horse.
'Who is that child?' he demanded. 'Surely we are not in
such sore straits for men that we must call upon such as he
to ride with us?' When word was brought back to him
that the child was none other than his own nephew Gui, he
was at first angry. Then, proud of the boy's courage, and
brushing away a tear, he said gruffly, 'Let him remain to
fight with us, if that is as he wishes.'

31

Meanwhile, at the court of the Emperor, Blanchefleur had repented of her jealousy and was urging Louis to send help to Guillaume. This at last he did, and so it was with a large army and in hope of victory that Guillaume once again met the Saracens in battle.

Before the first charge, he said to Gui, 'It were best you took no part in the fighting, for you are young and untried. How say you to watching the battle from yonder hill?'

'I would not consider such a thing!' replied Gui indignantly.

Guillaume smiled. 'Then keep close to me,' he ordered. 'We will fight side by side as true comrades in arms.'

And all through the battle Gui kept close to his uncle, and proved himself, though young and small, as brave as any man. 'You have a warrior's heart in the body of a boy,' said Guillaume; and Gui's pride and joy were unbounded.

This time the Saracens were utterly defeated, and they fled from Aquitaine; and Guillaume and little Gui returned home to Orange in triumph, where Guibourg greeted them joyfully. And at last the Emperor Louis recognized the worth of Guillaume, and admitted that he had no nobler vassal nor one more loyal, and gave him all Aquitaine for his own. And there in Aquitaine Guillaume Shortnose ruled wisely for many years, helped and encouraged by his faithful Guibourg.

Raoul of Cambrai

THERE was in the days of Charlemagne a brave knight named Taillefer, and for his services the Emperor rewarded him with the town of Cambrai, to the north of France, and all the land that lay round about. In the time of the Emperor Louis, who succeeded his father Charlemagne, Taillefer died, leaving a fair young widow, Aalais, and a new born son, Raoul. Aalais was sad at the loss of her lord, but she was a brave and proud lady, and she determined that her little son should grow up strong and valiant and worthy of the wide lands that were his.

But the Emperor Louis had a knight named Gibouin who had fought long and well for him in his wars, and he wished to reward him. He looked about all France for a fief that he might give to him, and he saw the lands around Cambrai, ruled by a woman and a babe. 'I will give you the lands of Cambrai,' he said to Gibouin, 'and you shall marry the widowed Lady Aalais.'

So on a day when Raoul was but three years old, a messenger came to Cambrai from Louis, bidding Aalais make ready to wed with Gibouin. But Aalais had loved her lord, and she would see no other in his place, so with anger and with indignation she refused to obey the Emperor.

'If you may not have the lady, you shall at least have the lands,' said Louis to Gibouin. And he seized all the lands that had belonged to Taillefer, all save the castle of Cambrai itself, where Aalais lived with Raoul, and gave them to Gibouin. Thus, at three years old, was young Raoul disinherited by the foolish Emperor.

In the castle of Cambrai, denied nothing by his mother, Raoul grew up into a handsome youth, tall and brave, but ever headstrong and over-fond of having his own way. He learnt knightly feats and conduct from his uncle, Guerri the Red, and his constant companion was Bernier, son of a nobleman named Ybert, who had sent the boy to Cambrai to be Raoul's squire.

When Raoul was fifteen years old, he bade farewell to his mother and rode to Paris to ask knighthood of the Emperor. And with him went Bernier to wait upon him. When Louis saw how fine a youth Raoul was, he knighted him willingly and gave him a sword and other gifts besides, and bade him remain at court for as long as he would. But in his good fortune at the Emperor's favour, Raoul did not forget his friend Bernier. He bought him arms and armour, the best that he could find, and a fine war-horse, and he made him a knight. And Bernier knelt before Raoul and laid his hands in his and swore allegiance to him for ever. Raoul remained at court for several years, serving the

Emperor with loyalty, but in his heart only waiting until he might ask him to give back his inheritance.

When it was seen how the Emperor favoured Raoul, many noblemen sent their young sons to serve him as squires, and among them were the two sons of Count Ernaut. One Easter day, after they came out of the church of St Denis in Paris, Raoul and his knights and squires began to tourney in the field before the church. But in the game some angry words were spoken, and the sport turned to earnest, and in the fighting the two sons of Ernaut were slain. For this Count Ernaut blamed Raoul, and swore one day to be avenged on him.

There came a day when Raoul had been at court for five years or more, and he went to the Emperor and said, 'Sire, I have served you faithfully since first I bore arms. Give me now as a reward my father's lands, which should rightly be my own.'

But Louis answered, 'I gave them as a gift to my knight Gibouin. I cannot take them from him.'

Raoul grew angry, and he spoke proud words to the Emperor, demanding his lands; and Louis, weak and foolish, was torn between his gratitude to Gibouin and his affection for young Raoul, and at last he said, 'I cannot give you back your father's lands, but if you will be patient for a few months longer, I promise you that I will give to you the lands of the next of my vassals to die. For I know now that I have wronged you grievously, and I would it were righted.'

Raoul considered the Emperor's offer and sought counsel of his uncle, Guerri the Red, and Guerri bade him accept. Raoul returned to the Emperor, agreed to the offer, and took hostages from him that he should keep his word.

When but a year was passed, old Count Herbert died, who had held all the land of Vermandois and the fair town of Origny, which lay to the south of Cambrai. As soon as Raoul heard of his death, he said to the Emperor, 'Give me now Vermandois and Origny and the lands of Court Herbert, as you promised me.'

But Louis grew pale and wrung his hands. 'Count Herbert had four sons. How can I disinherit four men for the sake of one?'

Raoul was beside himself with anger. 'I have your hostages,' he cried. 'Do you not care what becomes of them?'

And at last Louis, distressed and fearful, yielded. 'I will not deny you Vermandois and Origny and the lands which were Count Herbert's. But you will get no help from me in the winning of them. And I warn you that Herbert's sons are powerful men, with many friends, and they will defend their rights.'

'I care nothing for them or their friends, and I shall take the lands that you have given me,' said Raoul.

Now, the sons of old Count Herbert were Ybert, Wedon, Herbert, and Louis. Ybert was the eldest, and he was the father of Bernier. When Bernier learnt that Raoul meant to fight for the land of Vermandois, he knelt before his friend and pleaded with him. 'Do not break peace with the sons of Herbert, for they are very powerful, and it will go ill with you.' But Raoul only gave him scornful words in reply.

36

Raoul rode home to Cambrai to call together all the men who would fight for him; but when his mother heard how he would make war upon the sons of Count Herbert she grew pale. 'Dear son, I beg of you, leave this madness. Old Count Herbert was ever a good friend to your father Taillefer. What harm had he done to you?'

'This thing is the fault and the folly of the Emperor, not mine, but what I have undertaken, I shall complete.' And Raoul would not listen to her nor to any other who sought to dissuade him from his course, though of them all, only Guerri the Red, who loved battles and fighting, gave him encouragement.

When Raoul had called together all who would carry arms for him, he had barely ten thousand men, and of these, few were proved knights, and many had offered their swords only in the hope of gain, and many were cowards who feared Raoul's wrath if they held back from the enterprise.

'The sons of Herbert will have five men to each one of yours, my son,' said the Lady Aalais, 'and they will all be tried warriors. For the last time, I beg of you, give up this madness of yours.'

'War is no matter for a woman,' said Raoul. 'Go back to your spinning, mother, and trouble me no more.'

Aalais grew angry, so that she did not know what she spoke. 'If you will not do what I ask for love of me, then go, and may you never see your home again.' And she wept.

Raoul, at the head of his army, with Guerri as his standard bearer, rode south from Cambrai to the land of

Vermandois; and, heavy at heart, Bernier rode with him, because he loved his friend, and because he had sworn to serve him till he died.

In Vermandois, Raoul burnt down farms and crops and laid waste the countryside as far as the town of Origny. And there before the walls of the town, in a wide meadow, he pitched camp. 'Tomorrow,' he said, 'we attack the town.' And Bernier's heart grew even heavier, for in the convent of Origny his mother, Marsent, was a nun.

In the morning the assault upon the walls began, but Bernier remained in his tent, and would not arm himself. Eagerly Raoul led the attack upon Origny; but when it seemed as though the town must fall, the gates opened, and the nuns from the convent came out to plead with him, and Marsent asked to speak with Raoul.

'What will you of me, lady?' he asked.

'We have done you no harm, Lord Raoul, we are peaceable folk in this town. Spare us and give us a truce. We who ask in the name of the others are nuns. No ill have we ever done to any, we bear no weapons, through our deeds no man has ever lost his life. For the love of God's Son who died for all of us, since tomorrow is Good Friday, have mercy on the people of Origny and give us a truce.'

Raoul thought for a while and then he said, 'You have spoken well, lady. For your sake I will give the town a truce.' And he called off his men and rode back to the camp.

Bernier came to his mother, who had not seen him since he had been a tiny child, and she embraced him and rejoiced to see how handsome and how strong he was. 'This

Raoul whom you serve,' she asked, 'is he a good man or no?'

Bernier sighed. 'He is wild and unbridled, and there is a madness on him in this thing, but all I have I owe to him: my horse, my arms, my armour, and it was he who made me a knight. He is my friend, and I must serve him until I can serve him no longer.'

Marsent smiled a little. 'My blessing be on him,' she said, 'for all that he has done for you.'

Among Raoul's men there were many who, having followed him for gain, were disappointed at the truce, for they had hoped for much loot when the town was taken. As these men grumbled together, three rogues among them stole away in the darkness and climbed over the walls of the town, and laying hands on all they could find, made their way back again towards the camp. But they were spied by the watch and were pursued, and being laden with their spoils, two of them were caught and slain. But the other threw down the goods which he had stolen, and so escaped. Then, before any might accuse him, he went to Raoul's tent, and flinging himself at his feet, told how he and two companions had been set upon outside the camp by the men of Origny. 'My friends were slain, lord, and I alone escaped. I beg of you, avenge this violation of the truce.'

Raoul, believing him, leapt up in great anger, and swore to burn the town. At dawn he attacked, and all unprepared, the town fell easily; and at Raoul's orders his men swept through the streets, burning and slaying and taking great booty.

The nuns fled from their convent to the safety of the

church; but not even the church was spared, and in the flames all the nuns perished. And Bernier, coming with haste, too late to save her, found his mother Marsent dead. 'How can I forgive Raoul for this?' he thought.

Raoul returned to his camp, well pleased at the vengeance he had taken on Origny, and in his tent he called for a feast to be prepared, that he might celebrate his victory. 'Let us have roasted peacocks and venison and plump swans, and let every man eat his fill.' But his seneschal cried out in horror, 'Lord, have you forgotten that it is Lent, and that we may not feast? And more, this is the day on which our Saviour died for us. God have mercy on us all for what we have done today.'

Raoul answered him angrily. 'The people of Origny broke the truce, they brought their fate on themselves.' He shrugged his shoulders. 'Yet I had forgotten what day it was. We will not feast. Let one of you play chess with me, for I would be diverted.'

Sullen and unsmiling, Raoul sat before his tent, his chair set upon the green grass of the meadow, and played chess with one of his knights. And while he played he called for wine. There were several who ran to do his bidding, yet it was Bernier who filled a golden cup, and bringing it, knelt beside his lord to offer it. But Raoul was intent upon the chessmen, and he did not notice him, until Bernier, angry at Raoul for the grief that he had caused him, and thinking himself slighted, said, 'By all the saints, if you will not take the wine you have asked for, I will pour it away on the ground.' And there were many present, who, hearing him, trembled at his presumption.

Yet Raoul turned quickly, and seeing Bernier, smiled and spoke kindly. 'Good friend, truly I did not see you there.' And he stretched out his hand for the cup. Then, his mood lightened by the presence of his friend, he spoke boastfully to his knights gathered about his tent. 'By this good wine, and by my sword, I swear to you all that the sons of Count Herbert will be in a sorry plight when I have done with them.'

'You will have need of great good fortune,' said Bernier quietly, 'for they have more than fifty vassals pledged to fight for them.'

Raoul paid no heed to his words. 'I will kill them, all four of them, or drive them into exile over the sea, and their lands shall be mine.'

Bernier, standing before Raoul, spoke bitterly. 'You are a brave man, Raoul, but ill have you done today. You have killed my good mother, and now you would kill my father and my uncles. And yet here am I who should be fighting at their side: your liegeman, in your company, among your knights.'

Angered, Raoul answered, though in his heart he knew it was not true, 'How am I to know that you are not fighting for them at this very moment, spying on me that you may betray me to my enemies? If I were wise, I would slay you now.'

'This is a fine reward for my service and my love, Raoul, that you doubt me now. I am alone here, with neither brother nor kinsman, yet I am ready to fight against any man to prove I am no spy. And when I am armed, with my good sword in my hand, there will be few who dare to oppose me. Even you, Raoul, might lack the courage to match yourself with me.'

At Bernier's words, beside himself with rage, Raoul leapt to his feet, and snatching up a lance which lay upon the grass close by, with the shaft of it he struck Bernier across the head, so that the blood streamed down his face.

'This,' said Bernier, 'is the last insult you shall offer me, for I shall be gone from your company for ever.' And he turned to go. But when Raoul saw that he would lose his friend, his anger left him, and he was sorry for his words and the blow he had struck. 'Bernier, we have ever been as brothers, you cannot leave me now. Pardon me and I will make amends to you before all men.' Yet Bernier gave him no answer. Then Raoul, for all his pride and haughtiness, knelt down before Bernier and pleaded for forgiveness. 'I would lose all I own,' he said, 'sooner than I would thus shame myself before any other man, yet you I cannot lose.'

But Guerri the Red called out, 'However my nephew Raoul feels in this matter, I shall ever be against you, traitor Bernier, for your treason towards him.'

'This,' said Bernier quietly, 'is the end of my allegiance.' And he went to his own tent and bound a cloth about his wounded head, and armed himself; then he rode from the camp.

Bernier went to where his father, Ybert, whom he had not seen for many years, and his uncles Wedon, Herbert, and Louis, with their friends and vassals, had gathered together their army to protect their lands from Raoul, and he told them of all that had passed. Immediately they set out for Origny, with fifty thousand men. And among their friends was Count Ernaut, who had blamed Raoul for the death of his young sons, eager for his vengeance.

When they came within sight of Origny, Wedon said, 'Let us not be rash in this matter. The Emperor is a good friend to Raoul; it would be perhaps wise were we to ask for peace before we begin war.' So a messenger was sent to Raoul's camp, bidding him withdraw his men to Cambrai and leave the sons of Herbert their inheritance.

'It is a fair offer, nephew,' said Guerri. 'Their men outnumber ours.'

'Though you may be a coward, my uncle, I am none,' replied Raoul. 'I am ready to fight for the lands the Emperor has given me.' And he bade the messenger depart.

When Wedon heard the answer, he shook his head. 'Raoul is young and hasty and impetuous. Moderation becomes men in all things, and peace is better than war. Let us send to him once again, my brothers; he may perhaps have changed his mind.'

'Let us have done with talking,' said Ybert, 'for we have much to avenge.' But Wedon's counsel prevailed, and the four brothers agreed to send to Raoul once more.

'Let me be your messenger this time,' said Bernier. And he rode alone to Raoul's camp and spoke to Raoul. 'My father and my uncles have sent me to offer you peace once again. If you will accept their terms and quit their lands and return to your own castle of Cambrai, I for my part will accept your amends for the slaying of my mother, for the blow you struck me, and for the insults which you offered me.'

43

Raoul's heart lightened at the thought that he and Bernier might yet be accorded. 'That is the offer of a friend,' he said, 'and I should do well to accept it.'

But Guerri the Red, who had ever given his nephew bad counsel, spoke scornfully. 'You named me a coward when I called the offer fair. Who is the coward now? By all means, nephew, flee to Cambrai and hide yourself and leave me to fight alone.'

'If you fight, good uncle, I must fight beside you.' Raoul turned to Bernier with a sigh. 'Then it must be war between us,' he said.

Bernier shrugged his shoulders. 'I am glad of it, for thus I may avenge my mother.' And he rode back to his father and his uncles.

Ybert spoke to his fifty thousand men. 'Ours is the just cause. Let us go forward.' And they rode towards Origny.

Raoul and Guerri the Red at the head of their men rode to meet them and the battle was joined. Raoul and his uncle fought bravely, close beside each other, promising to keep together throughout all the fighting, that they might be a sure defence to one another. On both sides many men were slain, and in the press of battle all the four sons of Herbert, and Ernaut, who wished to avenge his sons, sought everywhere for Raoul.

It was Ernaut who found him first and called out bitterly to him, reproaching him with the death of the boys. 'It was not my fault they died,' said Raoul as they rode at one another. They fought together fiercely, and many hard blows they gave each other, until with a stroke of his

44

sword Raoul cut off Ernaut's left hand, so that he could no longer hold his shield. Ernaut grew afraid, seeing death so close, and he turned his horse and fled. Raoul, forgetting his promise to his uncle, galloped after, and his horse was better than Ernaut's, so that he gained on him. Ernaut in his fear called out, offering Raoul all his lands if he would only spare his life. 'I would rather see you lying dead,' said Raoul. Ernaut, still fleeing for his life, called out for aid, and Raoul taunted him. 'There is no one can help you now, Count Ernaut, neither man nor saint, nor even God Himself.'

'You have spoken blasphemy,' said Ernaut, 'and God will punish it.' Then, because his horse could go no farther, he turned to face Raoul, his sword in his hand. But Bernier had heard his cries for help, and he came riding fast, calling out to Raoul, 'Let him be, he is half dead already. Oh, Raoul, once my friend, make your peace with my kinsmen and let this battle be done.'

'You plead well,' answered Raoul, 'but it is now too late.' He rode against Bernier, and each struck the other such a heavy blow that their shields were shattered. Then Bernier lifted up his sword and brought it down with all his might on Raoul's head, so that his helmet was broken and the sword cut through to the bone. Raoul dropped his sword and swayed in his saddle and fell to the ground. He tried to stand, and took hold of his sword, but he had not the strength to raise it up, nor could he see where Bernier was, and the sword slipped from his hand on to the grass. 'How ill-fated was the Emperor's gift,' he whispered. 'God have mercy on me now.'

45

'I have had my vengeance,' said Bernier, 'and I no longer desire it.'

Count Ernaut laughed. 'Now my one hand shall avenge the other.' He rode forward and raised his sword.

'It is no knightly deed, to kill a dying man,' said Bernier.

'I have great cause to hate him.' Ernaut leant from his horse and struck Raoul upon the head, then lifting up his sword once more, he drove it through his heart. 'Now are you killed indeed, Raoul, who brought so much grief to so many.' And Ernaut rejoiced in his triumph.

But Bernier wept, because his friend was dead. 'Would God I had not done it,' he said.

FRENCH COURTLY TALES OF
THE MIDDLE AGES

Aucassin and Nicolette

Long ago there ruled in Beaucaire an old count who had but one child, his son Aucassin, a comely youth with grey eyes and curling golden hair. Gracious he was, and generous, and of great courtesy, as a youth of noble birth should be; but for those other qualities which become the son of a count he cared nothing. He never rode a-hunting, he never donned helmet and hauberk to joust, on the tourney field and in the tilting yard he was never seen, and for the honours of knighthood he had no wish. But ever would he spend his days in the company of the maiden whom he loved; or when that might not be, he would sit alone and dream of her.

In the city of Beaucaire the Count had a vassal who, fifteen years before, knowing nothing of her birth or parentage, had out of pity bought from Saracen pirates a little girl. He had baptized this child and called her Nicolette, and brought her up with kindness in his own house, intending, when she came of an age to be married, to give her as a wife to some honest man-at-arms or merchant. But Aucassin had once seen Nicolette and loved her straightway, so that he cared for nothing else, and at all hours of every day he would be at the vassal's house, seeking speech with Nicolette; and for her part, she was very glad of this.

The Count of Beaucaire was ill pleased by his son's love for a maiden who had once been sold as a slave and about whom nothing else was known, and he spoke to him of marriage with one of his own rank, the daughter of a count or a duke, or even of a king. But Aucassin answered him, 'I will have Nicolette for my wife, or no one else.'

Angered, the Count bade his vassal send Nicolette far off where his son might no more see her. 'If you do not obey me in this,' he said, 'it will go ill with you. And as for this wretched girl, she shall be burnt.'

So the vassal, afraid, locked Nicolette away, with only an old woman for company, in a room at the very top of his house, with no more than one little window, looking down upon the garden.

When Aucassin found that Nicolette was gone, and no man could tell him where, he sought out his father's vassal and asked what had become of her. 'Lord,' said the vassal, 'it is your father's wish that you should see and speak with her no more.' And though Aucassin argued and pleaded with him, it was in vain. 'I fear the Count too much, lord. For if I disobey him in this matter, Nicolette will be burnt, and perhaps I also.'

So with a heavy heart Aucassin returned to his father's castle, cast himself down on his bed, and wept. And there he remained, sighing for Nicolette and paying no heed to any who sought to reason with him.

For some time the Count of Valence had waged war upon the Count of Beaucaire, and hardly a day had passed when he had not made an attack upon his lands. Since Aucassin's father was too old for fighting, often had he tried to persuade his son to lead the men of Beaucaire to battle. But caring for nothing save his love for Nicolette, Aucassin had taken no part in the war. But now there came a day when the Count of Valence said, 'This war has lasted long enough. We must make an end of it.' And with all his forces he attacked the city of Beaucaire, meaning not to cease until it was in his hands.

The Count of Beaucaire went to Aucassin, where he grieved, lying upon his bed. 'Are you a coward?' he asked. 'Or would you be shamed for ever, that you lie here, when, at any hour, our city may be taken? Rise up and put on your armour and lead our men to battle. It will give them fresh courage against the enemy, if they see you at their head.'

But Aucassin only answered, 'I care nothing for the city if I may not have my Nicolette.'

'And I would rather lose my city and all my lands, than see my son wedded with a maiden who comes from no one knows where.' The Count turned away in anger and would have left the room, but suddenly Aucassin sat up upon his bed. 'Father,' he said, 'let us make a bargain. If I do this thing for you, and put on my armour and lead out your men, when I return, will you let me see my Nicolette, and speak a word or two to her and give her one kiss?'

'I will do that,' said the Count.

Joyfully Aucassin put on armour and girded on a sword, taking up lance and shield with a merry heart. The gates of the city were opened, and on a huge war-horse, Aucassin rode out at the head of his father's men. But he gave not one thought to the battle or the enemy, remembering only his father's promise: how in a little while he would see Nicolette again. In his eagerness he spurred on his horse and it galloped forward, all alone, right to where the men of Valence stood thickest; and Aucassin, his eyes blind to all about him, saw only his Nicolette, and deaf to all else, heard only her sweet voice in his ears.

And then he came back to reality, to find himself surrounded by the enemy, his lance and his shield being dragged from his grasp, without his having struck one blow. Bewildered, he looked about him, while the men of Valence rejoiced and jeered. 'It is the son of the Count of Beaucaire. Let us take and hang him.' And they sent to their lord of Valence that he might see it done.

Then the thought suddenly came to Aucassin, 'If they hang me, I shall never see my Nicolette again.' He saw that they had not yet taken his sword from him, and before they knew what he was about, he had drawn it, and hacking and striking all around him, he won his way back towards the city. The Count of Valence, seeing his prize escaping, rode after him and sought to recapture him; but Aucassin fought mightily, thinking of his Nicolette, and he flung the Count from his horse and took him captive, dragging him into the city, to his father's feet.

'Here is your enemy, my father. See how I have ended

the war for you. Now quickly fulfil your promise and let me speak with Nicolette.'

'Might I be cursed if I kept to such a bargain,' said the Count of Beaucaire. 'If I had Nicolette before me now, I would order her burnt, that there might be an end to this foolish love of yours.'

When Aucassin saw how he had been cheated by his father, he released the Count of Valence from his bonds, gave him a horse, and saw him safely from the city. 'Let this be your ransom,' he said, 'that you never call my father friend.'

Then, in his wrath, the Count of Beaucaire had Aucassin cast into a dungeon, deep below a tower, where only one small barred window let in the light of day; and there he remained, weeping for his Nicolette.

One summer night soon after, as Nicolette lay unsleeping on her bed in the room where she was imprisoned, she thought of how the Count had sworn to burn her if he ever found her, and fearing lest he should discover where she had been hidden, she determined to escape and leave the city. So, hearing from her snores that the old woman who guarded her was sleeping, she rose quietly and dressed herself; then knotting together the sheets and the coverlet from her bed, she fastened one end of the rope she had made to the window-frame and climbed down into the garden. Lightly she ran across the garden, and out through the garden gate.

In the streets, wrapped in her dark cloak, she kept close to the houses, in the shadows, making for the city walls. In this fashion, by chance she came by the tower below which

Aucassin lay bound. Through the small window of his dungeon she heard his voice, sighing for her. She knelt down and spoke to him through the bars. 'Aucassin, dear love, it is I, your Nicolette. Since your father will never permit us to marry, and since he has sworn to kill me, should he ever find me, I am leaving the city to seek safety in another place.' And she cut off a tress of her hair and dropped it down to him.

'You will go to another land, and there another man will make you his wife, and I shall die for love of you,' said Aucassin.

'Alas,' said Nicolette, 'what else can I do?' With tears they bade each other farewell, and Nicolette went on her way. She found a spot where the city walls had been damaged in the siege, and with great pain she climbed

them; and then with much labour and in fear she crossed the moat and somehow reached the other side, and made for the nearby forest. On the edge of the forest she hid among the bushes and slept, for she was very weary.

At dawn she awoke to the sound of voices, and coming out from her hiding-place, she saw three or four shepherd lads eating their breakfast. She went to them.

54

'Good shepherds, if Aucassin, the Count's son, should ever chance this way, tell him, I beg of you, that in this forest there is a fair quarry for his hunting, such that he would not part with for five hundred golden marks.'

They stared at her, and one of them answered, 'There is no beast in all this forest worth one golden mark. You must be out of your mind, or a fairy woman, to speak such words. But should the Lord Aucassin ride this way, I will tell him what you said.'

Nicolette thanked him and went on into the forest, and there, among the trees, she built herself a bower of leaves and branches.

When he found that Nicolette was gone from his house, the Count's vassal went to his lord and said, 'I have done as you bade me, and Nicolette is no longer in my keeping.' And thinking her to have been sent far away, the Count was glad, and in his gladness forgave his son and released him from the dungeon. Aucassin mounted a horse and rode out of the city and away to the forest, to be alone with his grief. On the edge of the forest he came upon the shepherd lads, and they spoke to him. 'Are you not Lord Aucassin, the son of our Count?'

'I am,' he said.

'There has passed this way,' said one of the shepherds, 'a maiden, be she mortal or fairy I know not, who left a strange message for you. She said that in this forest there is a quarry for your hunting, such as you would not part with for five hundred golden marks. Yet I cannot tell what she meant by her words.'

But Aucassin knew at once that it was Nicolette they

spoke of, and hopefully he rode on into the forest. All day he searched, and that night he came upon the bower she had built, and found Nicolette herself within. Their joy in being together once again knew no bounds, but Nicolette said, 'We cannot stay here, for if your father sends his men to search for you, and they find me with you, I shall be taken and burnt.'

'In the morning,' said Aucassin, 'we shall go far from my father's lands.'

At dawn he mounted his horse, set Nicolette before him, and together they rode from Beaucaire, and away to the coast. There they found a ship setting sail for a foreign land. They went aboard her and soon reached the island of Torelore, where they were welcomed by the King. And there they dwelt happily for a time.

But there came a day when the fleet of the King of Carthage raided the island, taking much booty and many prisoners to sell as slaves. And amongst those they took were Aucassin and Nicolette. Nicolette was led to the ship of the King of Carthage himself, while Aucassin was taken on board another vessel. When the spoils and prisoners were all bestowed, the fleet set sail for Carthage; but once out at sea, a storm arose. Blown from her course, and parted from the other vessels, the ship which carried Aucassin was wrecked upon the coast of France, close by the county of Beaucaire. Aucassin was saved by some fisher folk, and from them he learnt that his father was dead, so that he was now the Count and ruler of Beaucaire. He went at once to his own lands and was received with great joy, for all had thought him dead. His vassals came to do him homage, and in all his realm was peace and happiness; but his own heart was heavy, for he did not know what had become of Nicolette.

Yet indeed, no ill had come to her, for when the King of Carthage and his twelve sons saw her, for some reason they could not guess, she seemed familiar to them, and they held her in all honour and questioned her as to who she was and whence she came. But all she could tell them was that she had been stolen from her home by pirates when she was a very little child and had since lived in Beaucaire. After several days at sea, the coast of Carthage came in sight, and as soon as she saw the harbour and the buildings and the country that lay round about, Nicolette cried out that she had seen it all before. And the King of Carthage embraced her, saying, 'You will be my lost daughter, who was stolen from me, fifteen years ago.'

He took her to his palace, giving her rich clothes to wear and costly gifts, and he looked about him at all his noblest lords, seeking a husband worthy of her. But Nicolette thought only of how she might return to Aucassin. And when a means had come into her mind, she asked that she might learn to play the lute, and it was granted her. When she had mastered the art, she cut off her hair and stained her skin with walnut juice, and in the garb of a boy she slipped from the palace and down to the harbour. There she sought out the captain of a ship that was to go to France, and asked to sail with him. And because she sang sweetly and played so well upon the lute, he gave her passage willingly, and set her ashore on the coast of Provence.

From there she travelled as a minstrel to Beaucaire, to

see if she might hear news of Aucassin; and in the city of Beaucaire she found that he ruled as count, his father being dead. But she had no way of telling whether he still loved her, so, going to the castle, she asked if she might sing before the Count.

She played upon her lute and sang a song that she had made, of the love of Aucassin and Nicolette: how they had fled away together, and how they had been parted, and how Nicolette was the daughter of the King of Carthage. When the song was done, Aucassin called her to him and spoke to her apart. 'Sir minstrel,' he said, 'tell me what more you know of this lady, Nicolette.'

'Lord,' she said, 'I know that her father would give her as a wife to the highest in his land. But she would rather die than be the wife of any but the one she loves.'

'And I,' said Aucassin, 'will have no wife at all, unless I can have my Nicolette.' And he wept, remembering her.

And Nicolette, knowing that he still loved her, told him who she was, and in great joy he took her in his arms. And so at last they were married and lived long and happily in Beaucaire.

Huon of Bordeaux

A DUKE of Bordeaux died, leaving to succeed him his son Huon, a boy of no more than ten years old. Seven years later, it came to the mind of the Emperor of France that the young Duke had not yet paid homage for his lands. So the Emperor sent to Huon, bidding him come to Paris immediately to swear allegiance to his overlord, on pain of losing all his lands. Huon at once set out for Paris, accompanied by his younger brother, Gerard, and twenty knights.

Now, the lands of the dukedom of Bordeaux, in Gascony, were wide and rich, and they were coveted by the eldest son of the Emperor, an ambitious and dishonest man, who wondered how he might dispossess young Huon of them. He spoke of the matter to his friend Amauri, and together they planned to ambush Huon on his way to Paris and slay him, so that when he did not arrive at court it might appear to the Emperor that the young Duke had disobeyed him and, angered, he would seize his lands, for which the Prince would then ask his father.

Accordingly, with fifty knights they lay in wait beside a wood, a half-day's journey from Paris, and when Huon and his men came in sight, they prepared to attack. The Gascons rode gaily, fearing no treachery, and ahead of them cantered young Gerard, with his falcon on his wrist, excited at the thought of seeing the great city of Paris.

'I shall go alone,' said the Prince, 'so that seeing no more than one knight they will have no suspicions, and when I give the signal, do you, Amauri, come on with our men and slay them all.' The Prince rode out of the wood and set his horse right in Gerard's path. 'Not so fast, young stranger,' he said.

Gerard, resenting his words, answered him impatiently, 'By your leave, sir knight, I would pass,' and he made to thrust his way past the Prince. But with a blow of his lance, the Prince flung the boy from his horse, and Gerard shouted for help as he fell.

Huon spurred on his horse and came up to them, flushed and angry. 'That was basely done, to strike an unarmed boy who had done you no harm.'

'Have a care for yourself also,' sneered the Prince, and he lowered his lance at Huon and rode at him. Huon managed to avoid the blow, then, impetuous like all Gascons, without wasting another word, he drew his sword and struck at the Prince; and for all his youth, so mighty was the blow that the Prince's helmet and his head were both shattered, and the Emperor's favourite son fell dead. 'A fine welcome to Paris,' said Huon, as his men caught up with him, 'to be set upon by a robber knight.'

When Amauri and the fifty knights saw how the Prince was slain, they did not leave the shelter of the woods, but waited until Huon and his men had bound up Gerard's hurt and ridden on. Then Amauri took up the body of his friend and laid it over his saddle bow and rode slowly back to Paris.

Meanwhile, Huon came before the Emperor, who received him kindly and heard with anger his story of the robber knight. 'That was a shameful deed,' he said, 'and well did such a wretch deserve his death.'

But then came Amauri with the Prince's body, and he laid it at the Emperor's feet. 'Your dear son is dead, sire, and it was Huon of Bordeaux who forced a quarrel on him and slew him before he could defend himself.'

In his great rage and sorrow the Emperor snatched up a sword and would have slain Huon where he stood, had not his courtiers prevented him. 'Sire, do not kill him before he has a chance to speak,' they pleaded.

For a long time the Emperor would not listen to Huon's protestations that he had neither known who the Prince was nor struck the first blow, and that Amauri was lying; but at last he agreed that Huon should meet Amauri in single combat, to prove which of them spoke the truth.

Seeing Huon's youth, Amauri was confident of being the victor, but Huon was no mean jouster, and he was, moreover, very angry. He rode against Amauri, striking furiously, and so unexpected were his blows and so agilely he fought, that Amauri was overcome and Huon in triumph struck off his head.

But the Emperor had loved his son dearly, and he had always trusted him and believed him honourable, so that he was not satisfied, and for all the pleading of his lords he could not find it in his heart to pardon Huon. Finally he said, 'I will grant you my forgiveness when you have achieved a certain task for me. Go to the city of Babylon, where the great Saracen Emir rules, and there, in the Emir's palace, before his eyes, kill the most exalted of the guests who sit to eat with him; give three kisses to his daughter, the Princess Claramunda; and bring me the Emir's beard and four of his teeth. Only if you fulfil these conditions will I pardon you.'

Sadly Huon bade farewell to his brother and his knights and set off on the long journey to Babylon. In the seventeen years of his life he had never left France, and he wondered how far he would be able to travel on his quest before he was slain by the Saracens for a Christian, or captured and sold as a slave. He crossed the sea to the Holy Land and rode on across the wild and barren desert into Syria, and from there went on towards Babylon, and many were the adventures he had on the way.

One day, in a vast forest, he came upon a dwarf with a face of unearthly beauty, Oberon, the king of the fairy world. Oberon greeted Huon kindly, and at a word brought to being in the forest a palace of unsurpassed magnificence, where his guest was attended by unseen servants and offered every comfort he could desire. In this palace Huon passed the night, and in the morning, at Oberon's command, it vanished away, and Huon was once more in the dark and gloomy forest. 'Before we part,' said Oberon to him, 'I would give you a gift which will help you on your quest.' He took from about his neck a horn of ivory. 'When you are in danger, sound this horn, and I will come to you. But remember well that it is only to the aid of a true and honourable knight that I will come. If you should at any time have told a lie to save your life, then do not call on me.'

'May I never prove unworthy of your gift,' said Huon as he took the horn and bade Oberon farewell.

On another day, in a brazen tower which was guarded by two men of bronze who wielded two great flails like the sails of a windmill, Huon overcame and slew a giant named Angoulafre and took from him his huge ring.

But finally, all the perils of the journey safely passed, and the last and greatest danger of all awaiting him, Huon came to Babylon, a rich and wondrous city. He made his way to the palace, and there he found the Emir's guests arriving for the betrothal feast of the Princess Claramunda and the Prince of Hyrcania. Huon watched the Saracen princes and lords pass through the gates, and then he boldly made to follow them; but the guards, seeing his Frankish armour and his fair complexion, barred his way with their weapons and challenged him. 'Only believers may feast with the Emir today.'

Impatiently Huon tried to thrust their spears aside. 'Let me pass,' he demanded.

'Do you acknowledge the Prophet?' asked the guards.

And Huon, hardly listening to the question, and only intent upon entering the palace, now that the end of his quest was in sight, answered, 'Yes,' and hurried by. Immediately afterwards, he realized what he had said, but rashly hastened on, along marble corridors, past cool fountains, into the banqueting hall. Here the Emir and his guests reclined upon cushions, served by slaves with cool drinks and the choicest meats. From the doorway Huon watched, and saw how on the right hand of the Emir sat his most honoured and exalted guest, thin-lipped and with a cruel smile, the Prince of Hyrcania, who was to marry his daughter; and on his left hand, the only woman there, her eyes above her veil bright with unshed tears, the Princess Claramunda.

Huon strode forward to where the Emir sat. 'I bring you greetings, my lord Emir, from the Emperor of France. Thus did my Emperor bid me do.' Huon drew his sword and with one stroke cut off the head of the Prince of Hyrcania, even before the thin lips had time to cease their smiling. The guests leapt to their feet in confusion, the servants fled in terror, and the Emir stared at Huon, unable to move for his surprise.

But for all her fear at the unexpected slaying, Claramunda had a moment of thankfulness as she realized that she would now never be the bride of the cruel Prince of Hyrcania; and then Huon had sheathed his sword and was standing before her. 'By your leave, lady,' he said, and put her veil aside. She was even lovelier than he had imagined she would be, but he had no time to spare for admiring her. Quickly he kissed her three times upon her lips and turned again to the Emir. 'Thus also did my Emperor bid me do.

And this did he bid me ask of you: that you will give to me your beard and four of your teeth.'

The Emir had by now recovered from his astonishment, and enraged, he arose, calling for his guards. 'Seize this madman and fling him in the dungeons,' he shouted.

'You would do well to have a care of me,' said Huon. 'It is best to have me as a friend, not as an enemy. Not so many days past, alone I slew the giant Angoulafre. See, here is his ring in proof of it.' And he held out the ring he had taken from the giant in the brazen tower.

The Emir saw it in amazement, for the giant had been known and dreaded far and wide, but he only called the more loudly for his guards, bidding them bring chains to bind their prisoner. Seeing them running towards him along the hall, Huon took the ivory horn that Oberon had given him and blew a loud blast on it. He blew again and yet again, but there was no sign from the fairy king; and then Huon remembered how he had answered the guards at the palace gates. 'I lied to save my life,' he thought, 'though I did not mean to do so. Oberon will not come.' He drew his sword again and set his back to the wall and prepared to fight alone against them all. He killed many of the Saracens before he was overpowered and disarmed; and when, hung with chains, he was finally dragged away to a dungeon beneath the palace, Claramunda wept, thinking how brave he was and how handsome, and how he had dared so much to kiss her.

All that night and throughout the next day, Huon lay on the cold stones of the dungeon floor and thought how he would never see Gascony again. 'The Emperor's son is well avenged,' he said to himself. Then late that evening, the key turned in the lock of the door and someone came in with a lantern. When Huon looked up, he saw that it was the Princess Claramunda. 'I have brought you food and water,' she said shyly. While he ate and drank thankfully, they talked. 'I have bribed the gaoler,' she said. 'We can trust him. I shall come with food again to-morrow.'

True to her word, she came each day; and one morning, at her bidding, the gaoler went to the Emir and said, 'Lord, the Frankish knight is dead.'

'It is well,' said the Emir, satisfied.

But Claramunda came every day to Huon with food, and every day they found more joy in each other's company; and more sorrow too, for as their love grew, so did their unhappiness at Huon's plight, for neither he nor Claramunda could think of a way of escape.

But by a lucky chance, Huon was delivered from the dungeon. One morning a terrified messenger came to the Emir's palace with news of how the dreaded giant Agrapard, brother of that Angoulafre whom Huon had slain, was approaching the city of Babylon with demands for tribute, naming a huge sum of gold to be paid to him if the Emir could not find a champion to do battle with him. In vain the Emir appealed to his lords and his warriors; but no one of them dared to meet the giant, and faced with the loss of all his riches, he wailed and tore his hair. 'If the Frankish knight who slew his brother had not died, my father,' said Claramunda, 'you would have a champion to face even the mighty Agrapard.'

66

'If only he were alive. If only I had not starved him,' groaned the Emir.

Claramunda flung herself at his feet. 'My lord father, he is not dead. Send for him, offer him his life if he will fight with the giant, and I do not doubt that he will accept.'

The Emir was too thankful to ask any questions for the moment, and at once he had Huon brought to him and he offered, in his great fear, not only Huon's life but the hand of Claramunda, and his own beard and four of his teeth, as the Emperor of France had demanded, if he overthrew Agrapard.

So once again Huon fought against a giant, and once again, after a terrible battle, he was the victor; and at last he dragged Agrapard, wounded and bound, to the feet of the Emir upon his throne, where he had sat to watch the combat, safe in the midst of his guards. 'Now, my lord Emir,' said Huon, 'fulfil all you have promised.'

But once the danger was past, the Emir cared little for his promise. 'You shall have your life,' he said, 'but nothing else. Begone to your own land, unless you would return to my dungeons again.'

In vain Huon protested, then, his quick Gascon temper flaring up, he drew his sword upon the Emir, who called to the guards to seize him. Huon took Oberon's horn from about his neck and blew it, and this time Oberon answered the summons and came forthwith at the head of an invisible fairy army. 'We are here, Duke Huon,' he said. At a word of command, the spirits fell upon the Saracens, who fought wildly against foes they could not see, hacking and hewing, and even striking at each other in their terror and amazement, until they were utterly routed, and fled. And in the turmoil the Emir was slain, so that Huon was able to cut off his beard and pull out four of his teeth.

Claramunda had few tears to shed for the father who had failed to keep his promise to the man she loved, and she was only too happy to leave Babylon with Huon, and go with him to France. In Paris, though he still grieved for his son, the Emperor pardoned Huon, praising him for the courage he had shown on his quest; and joyfully Huon returned to his beloved Gascony, where he married Claramunda and they lived happily for many years.

Amis and Amile

IN the land of France, in the same month of the same
year, were born two children. The one was son to a
knight of Bericain, and the other was son to the Count
of Alverne. When they were two years old, it came into
the minds of their fathers that they should take their sons
to Rome to be christened by the Pope. From the castle of
Bericain and from the castle of Alverne they set forth; and
it happened that in the town of Lucca, on the road to Rome,
the Count and the knight met and exchanged words of
greeting, and each hearing that the other was bound on the
same errand, they continued on their way together.

At Rome the two children were christened by the Pope.
The son of the knight of Bericain was given the name of
Amis, while the son of the Count of Alverne was called
Amile; and the Pope gave each of them as a christening gift
a carved wooden goblet inlaid with gold, each goblet de-
corated alike so that one might not have told them apart.

From that day the two children were fast friends. They grew up into tall and handsome youths, of a height, and with hair of the same colour, so that, seeing them together, one would have taken them for brothers.

When they had both been knighted, their fathers by then being dead, they went together to the court of the King of France, and there they proved themselves so worthy of honour that the King took them into his service and made Amis his treasurer and Amile his seneschal. In time Amis married a maiden named Lubias, who, though well content to be mistress of his castle at Bericain, had little love for her lord, and, moreover, begrudged his friendship for Amile. But Amile secretly loved Belisant, the daughter of the King, though he dared speak no word of his love for her, since her father had it in his mind that she should marry a great prince, and thereby win for him an alliance with another kingdom.

One day Amis left the court to journey to Bericain to visit his lady, Lubias. As he went, he bade farewell to Amile, embracing him and saying, 'Dear friend, while I am gone, have a care that you do not betray your love for the Princess, for it will go ill with you if the King should learn of it.' And Amile assured him that he would be prudent.

But though he did not know it, the Princess herself loved Amile, and soon after Amis had gone to Bericain she contrived that she should be alone with Amile and tell her love to him. He was overjoyed, and they kissed and pledged their faith. And after that they met many times in secret, and thought themselves unobserved. But at the King's court there was a nobleman named Arderi who hated both Amis and Amile for the favour shown them by the King. This Arderi spied upon Amile and the Princess, then going to the King he said, 'Sir Amile is a traitor to you, for though no more than a count, he has dared to speak words of love to your daughter Belisant, and to kiss her.'

The King was angered and sent for Amile, telling him of Arderi's accusation. Too late, Amile remembered the warning of Amis. 'I have done no wrong,' he said. But Arderi challenged him to prove it in battle against himself, and Amile could not refuse. So a day was chosen on which they should meet before the King and all the court, that it might be shown which of them lied and which spoke the truth.

Immediately, Amile rode from the court, meaning to seek out Amis in Bericain and ask his counsel, but on the road he met his friend returning. In great agitation he told Amis what had befallen. 'What shall I do?' he asked. 'For I dare not fight with Arderi, since he speaks the truth and so in the sight of heaven his cause will be just. And I dare not swear that I am innocent of loving the Princess, for it would be a lie, and God and all His saints would punish me and give the victory to Arderi. Tell me, dear Amis, what shall I do?'

'Go to my castle of Bericain and hide yourself there until I send for you,' said Amis. 'I shall go to court and meet Arderi for you. We are of one height and one build, and wearing your armour, no man shall guess that I am not you. And I can swear in all truth that I have never spoken words of love to the Princess or kissed her.'

71

So Amis took Amile's quarrel upon himself and fought with Arderi, and after a grim and mighty battle he was at last the victor and he slew Arderi and so proved Amile innocent of the charge.

When the King saw how Amile, as he thought him to be, had justified himself, he was ashamed of having believed Arderi's story, and he called Amis to him and said, 'Sir Amile, I would offer you amends for my misjudgement, and the best I have to offer is not too much. If you would, I will give you my daughter for your wife, for you have fought valiantly today to save her name.'

Joyfully Amis received the offer on Amile's behalf, and kneeling, thanked the King for the great honour which he did him. Then he sent for Amile, and going a little way along the road to meet him as he journeyed from the castle of Bericain, spoke privately with him and told him everything, and Amile had not words enough to thank him.

And so Amile was married to the Princess Belisant, and when she learnt how Amis had fought in his place, she said, 'I shall ever be grateful to him, and one day maybe we can repay him.'

After a time Amis and Amile left the service of the King and returned to their own lands. In his castle of Alverne, Amile lived happily with Belisant, and two sons were born to them. But Lubias, the wife of Amis, was still jealous of her lord's great love for his friend Amile, though she hid her jealousy carefully.

One day a great and terrible grief fell upon Amis, for he was stricken with leprosy so that there was no cure for him,

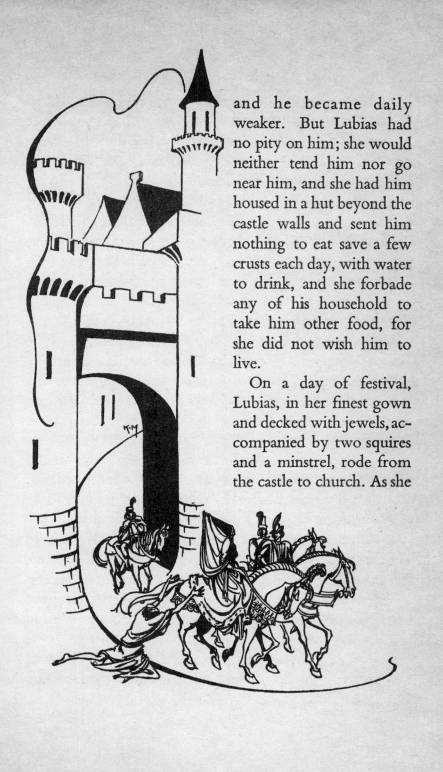

and he became daily weaker. But Lubias had no pity on him; she would neither tend him nor go near him, and she had him housed in a hut beyond the castle walls and sent him nothing to eat save a few crusts each day, with water to drink, and she forbade any of his household to take him other food, for she did not wish him to live.

On a day of festival, Lubias, in her finest gown and decked with jewels, accompanied by two squires and a minstrel, rode from the castle to church. As she passed by, Amis crept out of his miserable hut and called to her, pleading that she might show him a little kindness, and sometimes send him food from her own table, since he would soon be dead. 'The sooner you are dead, the sooner I shall be free of you,' said Lubias, and she rode on.

Amis sent for two of his servants who were still faithful to him, though they dared do little to help him for fear of Lubias, and he bade them lay him on a litter and carry him far from his castle. 'For,' he said, 'the world may have more pity on me than my own wife has shown.'

So the two servants set out with the dying man, and Amis took with him his leper's bell and the goblet which the Pope had given him at his christening, and he begged food and charity at all the houses that they passed. And at last, in this way, they came to the castle of Alverne, at a time when Amile was sitting down to eat. When he heard the leper's bell ringing in the courtyard, he said, 'It is a poor leper come for alms; take him out food and drink.' He heaped a plate with meat and bread and filled his own cup with wine and bade a servant take them out to the beggar. When the servant had done as he had been ordered, he came again to Amile and said, 'It is a strange thing, lord, but the beggar has with him even such a cup as yours, of carved wood and gold. I would have believed it yours, had I not been holding your own in my hand.'

Immediately Amile leapt up from the table and ran out to the courtyard, and there he saw his friend Amis, so wasted and changed by disease that at first he hardly knew him. He embraced him and wept. 'Is this the end of all our friendship,' he said, 'that you must die and I shall see you no more?' And he had Amis laid in his own bed and tended him himself, never leaving him by day or night.

One night as Amis was sleeping fitfully, he dreamt that he saw an angel who said to him, 'Amis, would you be cured of your leprosy?'

'I would that I might be cured, at whatever cost,' replied Amis.

'Then tell Amile your friend to slay his two children that you may wash in their blood, for only thus may you be cured.'

'That would I never ask of him,' said Amis, and he cried out the words in his sleep and awoke, so that Amile heard him and asked what ailed him.

'It was no more than a dream I had,' said Amis.

'Tell it to me,' said Amile. But Amis would not, yet he wept. Amile was troubled, and pressed him to tell his dream, so that at last Amis told it. 'But it was no more than a dream,' he said.

Amile comforted him and spoke gently to him until he fell asleep again, but he himself sat thinking until the dawn. Then he rose and went into the room where Belisant slept with their two sons. 'Rise up,' he said, 'and go to mass and pray for our friend Amis.' And when Belisant had gone, Amile took his sword and cut off his children's heads. Then with their blood he washed Amis, who was immediately cured of his leprosy, even as the angel had promised.

'Let us go to church and give thanks to God for His great mercy,' said Amile. He gave Amis his own finest garments to wear, and they went out from the castle together. As they entered the church they met Belisant coming forth, and her joy was plain when she saw Amis well and whole once more. Yet Amile thought, 'How shall I tell her that I have slain our sons to cure my friend?'

They all three gave thanks to God, and afterwards, in the castle, Belisant asked, 'How did this miracle come to pass?' and Amile told her. She grew very pale and wrung her hands together and turned away from him. But in a little while she turned to him again and said, 'That day he fought with Arderi, Amis did a matchless service for us. I have ever hoped that one day we might repay him. You should have told me, lord, what you had it in your mind to do to help our friend, so that I could have stood beside you and had my part in it.' But then she covered her face with her hands and wept, thinking of her children, and ran to the room where she had left them, dreading the sight she would find there. But when she came into the room she saw the two little boys sitting up in bed, laughing and playing together, quite unharmed, with only a thin red scar right around the neck of each to show how in the castle of Alverne two miracles had been done that day.

And for the rest of their lives Amis and Amile lived happily, and they died in the same hour.

The Grey Palfrey

IN the county of Champagne there once lived a knight. He was young and handsome and brave, and indeed he was all things that a good knight should be; but he was poor, owning little land and only one small manor set in a forest, among the trees and away from the road.

This young knight went much to the tourneying, often going many miles from his home to where tournaments were being held, not only for the sake of the honour he would gain by his courage and skill, but for the prizes and for the ransoms he might ask from those he overthrew, for it was by these ransoms that he lived and bought all that was needed for himself and for his servants and his few followers. Though his garments were always neat and his helmet and his hauberk polished bright, his clothes were plain and his armour none of the best, and the food he ate, though there was enough of it, was no rich fare.

But one thing this knight owned that would not have

shamed the wealthiest lord, and that was a grey palfrey, the favourite among his few horses, with sleek and glossy hide and a mane and a tail like flowing silver, so that no one, seeing it, did not stop to admire. Very fleet was this palfrey, and it had not its match in all Champagne. It was the envy of the countryside, and many were the rich lords who sought to buy it from the knight. Yet poor as he was, not for all the wealth in the world would he have parted with his palfrey, for he counted it his friend; and so indeed it proved to be.

Some two miles from this knight's manor, beside the road which ran through the forest, stood the castle of a duke. Old he was, and rich, and very miserly, forever seeking to add wealth to wealth. He had one daughter, the only young and gracious thing in all his castle, and it was this maiden whom the poor knight loved, and she loved him in return. But because he was poor, though of good repute, her father would never have considered him as a suitor; and since the maiden was never permitted to leave the castle, they might only speak together secretly, through a crack in the castle wall.

Every day at the same hour, when he was not at the tourneying, the knight would ride on the grey palfrey from his manor to the castle of the Duke, by a secret path through the forest which he alone used. And every day when she might, the maiden would await his coming at the castle wall, and they would talk of their love for a few happy moments. But not every day could she leave her father's side, or steal away unobserved, so on many days the knight would wait in vain to see her before riding sadly home along the secret path. Yet this made the times when they met all the sweeter.

One day the knight could bear it no longer, and since he knew the maiden cared nothing for riches, and would have been content as his wife had he been a peasant and lived in a hovel, he went to the castle and asked to speak with her father. The old Duke welcomed him courteously, since fair words cost nothing, and the young knight said, 'Lord, there is a favour I would ask of you.'

'And what might it be?' said the Duke.

'I am poor,' said the knight, 'but I am nobly born, and my honour is unquestioned, and no man has ever been able to speak ill of me. I love your daughter and I know that she loves me. I am here to ask for her hand in marriage.'

The old Duke went as pale as his white beard in his anger. 'There is not a lord in all France, nor a prince in all Christendom, whom I could not buy for my daughter, if I wished her to marry. She is not for a poor knight such as you. Now begone from my castle and never speak to me of such matters again.'

Heavy at heart, the knight rode home, but since the maiden loved him he did not lose all hope, and a day or two later he rode to a distant town where a great tournament was to be held, thinking that there he might win a small measure of those riches, which, if carefully saved, might cause the old Duke to relent.

At that time a lord, wealthy and old as the Duke himself, came to visit him, and after they had talked long together of the things they had done when young and the memories they had in common, the lord said, 'We are both rich, but were our riches combined, they would be even greater. Were you to give me your daughter as a wife, I would ask no dowry with her, but you and I, thus linked by a marriage, might share our wealth for the rest of our days. What say you to this, my old friend?'

The Duke was glad and rubbed his hands together and nodded many times. 'You have spoken well, it shall be as you say. In all France there will be none richer than we two.'

The Duke set about preparations for the marriage and cared nothing for his daughter's tears, inviting some score or more guests for the wedding, old friends of his and the bridegroom's, greybeards all. And because of his avarice, he sent to his neighbours in the countryside, asking the loan of a horse or two from each, that there might be mounts enough to carry the guests and their squires along the road through the forest to the church. And so little shame he had, that he sent to the young knight to borrow his grey palfrey, that his daughter might ride to her wedding on the finest horse in all Champagne.

The young knight had returned from the tourneying, well pleased enough with life, for he had easily been the best of all the knights gathered there, and every prize he had carried home to his little manor in the forest; so that it seemed to him he was perhaps a step nearer that which he had set his heart upon. When he heard the Duke's message, he asked, 'Why does your master wish to borrow my horse?'

And the Duke's servant answered, 'So that my master's

daughter may ride upon it tomorrow to her wedding at the church.'

When the young knight learnt how the maiden he loved was to marry the old lord, he thought that his heart would break, and at first he would have refused with indignation the Duke's request. But then he thought, 'Not for the sake of her father, but to do honour to the lady I love, will I lend my palfrey. It is I whom she loves, she will have no joy of this marriage, and perhaps it will comfort her a little if I send her the palfrey which is my friend.' So he saddled and bridled the palfrey and gave it to the serving-man, and then he went to his own room and would neither eat nor drink, but flung himself down upon his bed and wept.

In the Duke's castle, on the eve of the wedding, his guests made merry, feasting and drinking deep, and since they were, like himself, all old, when the time came for them to go to rest, they were in truth most weary. But very early in the morning, before dawn indeed, while the moon still shone brightly, the watchman roused them that they might be at the church betimes. Grumbling and half asleep, the guests clothed themselves and gathered in the courtyard where their horses waited. Yawning, they climbed into the saddles and set out upon their way, with the Duke and the old lord at their head. And after all the others came the maiden on the grey palfrey, with her father's old seneschal to watch over her. She was clad in a fair gown, and over it a scarlet mantle trimmed with costly fur, but her face was pale and she wept, and she had not slept all night for sorrow.

In the moonlight they left the castle and took the forest

road which led to the church; yet since the way was narrow and branches overhung the track, they might not ride two abreast, but followed each other one by one through the forest, with the old seneschal at the very end, after the weeping bride.

A little way along the road, from habit, the palfrey turned aside, taking the secret path that its master had so often used; and because the old seneschal was nodding and dozing as he rode, he never missed the maiden. Deep into the forest, along the secret way went the palfrey, and in terror the maiden looked about her. But though she was fearful, she did not cry out, for she thought, 'I had rather be lost in the forest and devoured by the wild beasts, than live without the knight I love.' And she let the palfrey carry her where it would.

After two miles, in the dim light of early dawn, the palfrey stopped before a small manor set among the trees and waited for the gate to be opened. The watchman peeped out through a grille and called, 'Who is there?' And, trembling, the maiden answered, 'I am alone and lost in the forest. Have pity on me and give me shelter till sunrise.'

But the watchman, looking closely, knew his master's palfrey, and made all haste to where he was. 'Lord,' he said, 'at the gate stands your palfrey, and on its back is a lady so lovely that I think she can be no mortal maid. Is is your will that I should let her in?'

The young knight leapt off his bed and ran to the gate and flung it wide and caught the maiden in his arms. When they had done with kissing and weeping for joy, he asked her, 'How did you come here?' And she answered, 'It was your grey palfrey that brought me, for I should not have known the way.'

'Since you are here,' said the knight, 'here shall you stay, if you will it.'

'It is all I ask, to be with you for ever,' she said.

So the knight called for his chaplain, and with no delay he and the maiden were married, and in all the manor there was great rejoicing.

When the Duke and the old lord and their friends reached the church they found that the maiden was not with them, and they set themselves to search for her, all about the forest. But by the time the Duke came upon the little manor set among the trees, his daughter was a wife, and there was nothing he could do about it, save give the marriage his blessing, which he did with an ill grace. But little the young knight and his lady cared for that.

Sir Lanval

THERE was in the service of a King of Brittany a poor knight named Lanval. He had neither lands nor riches, and he was, moreover, a stranger and had in all Brittany no single kinsman. He was handsome, courteous, and skilled in feats of arms and therefore much respected by his companions; but the King showed little gratitude to one who served him well and faithfully, and when there were lands and honours to be given, Sir Lanval was ever forgotten. Yet Lanval was loyal and spoke no word against the King, though the Breton knights were ashamed to see him slighted.

Lanval was generous and charitable with the little he owned, so there came a time when he had nothing left save his horse and his arms and his armour, and neither servant nor squire to serve him. And then his arms and his armour and his horse's trappings he sold to pay for his lodging, so that at last he had only the clothes he was wearing and his horse.

One summer morning, heavy at heart at the thought of his plight, he left his lodging to ride out to the fields beyond the city, that there, among the flowers and the green grass, he might forget for a little his troubles. The prentice lads laughed to see him ride through the streets in his threadbare cloak, with his horse stepping so proudly for all its worthless harness and the worn shoes on its feet; but Sir Lanval paid no heed.

Beyond the city walls, on the bank of a river, he drew rein and, the midday sun being hot, he dismounted, taking bit and bridle from his horse that it might crop the grass, for he had no money to buy fodder. Under the shade of a willow-tree Sir Lanval lay to rest, closing his eyes. After a a little time, hearing voices, he looked up and beheld approaching him two damsels, the fairest he had ever seen. They greeted him and said, 'Our mistress has bidden us bring you to her, for she would speak with you.'

'Willingly,' said Lanval courteously, 'shall I speak with her.' Then he saw, a little way off, a fair pavilion where, five minutes before, there had been none, and he followed the damsels amazed.

The pavilion was of many-coloured silk, with cords and tassels of silver thread and posts of gold, and well furnished within, so that even the richest king might envy it and never own a finer. And if the two damsels were beautiful, then there can be no words to describe their mistress, for she exceeded them by far, as the rose that grows in the garden surpasses the briar that climbs in the hedge; and her mantle was such as the Queen of Brittany herself did not own, of ermine and purple silk.

She welcomed Lanval kindly and bade him sit beside her. 'Sir Lanval,' she said, and her voice was sweet and gentle, 'I have come from far away in the fairy world, and it is for your sake that I have come. If you could find it in your heart to love me, even as I already love you, then I can give you riches and gifts and all that men desire.'

'Lady,' said Lanval, 'it is not for the riches and the gifts you offer me that I will love you, but for your own fair self. If you were a beggar-maid who asked for alms in the city streets, my heart would still be yours.'

She was joyful indeed when she heard his words. 'Well have I chosen the knight whom I love,' she said.

'Lady,' said Lanval, 'I will make no promises to you; for even if I would, I could love no other.'

Together they ate off golden dishes and drank from golden cups, served by the damsels; and all that day they had great joy in each other's company. When sunset was come, the lady said, 'It is time that you were gone. But whenever you would see me again, come to the bank of the river and call to me, and I shall be here, in my pavilion. But one thing I must demand of you, that you speak to no one of me or of our love, or I shall be lost to you for ever.'

'I would not share even the thought of you with any-one,' said Lanval.

She gave him a silken purse. 'In this,' she said, 'is fairy gold. No matter how much of it you spend, it will never be empty, and the more you spend, the more will there be to spend.' Lanval took the purse, bade her farewell, mounted his horse and returned to the city, marvelling at all that had befallen him.

86

Sir Lanval found that it was even as the lady had said, and the purse was never empty, but the more that he spent, the more there remained to spend. And soon he had rich clothes, the finest arms and armour in the city, servants to wait on him and squires to attend him. For the first time, he could feast his friends, and at last he might not stint in the giving of alms, and before long his charity and his kindness and his good fellowship were known throughout the city. No beggar or wandering minstrel was turned from his door, and he sought out all poor knights whose plight was as his own had been, that he might make them rich. And in all this time, whenever he went to the river and called upon her, there he would find his lady in her pavilion, and happy were the hours they enjoyed together.

When a year had passed since Lanval had first met the fairy woman, the King of Brittany, as was his custom, called all his lords and knights together for a feast on Whit Sunday, and to this feasting went Sir Lanval. While they ate and drank and laughed together, the King, being merry with wine, began to praise the beauty of the Queen. 'There is not a lovelier lady in all the world,' he boasted. And he bade her put off her royal robes and stand before them, that all the company might judge how fair she was. The Queen, being vain, was glad to do as she was bidden, and stand in the midst of the hall with all men's eyes upon her, admiring her. Yet though the Queen was fair enough, there were other ladies more lovely; but because she was the Queen, and because they sought to please the King, all the lords and knights cried out in admiration and said aloud how they had never seen so fair a lady. 'The King speaks truly,' they said. 'Surely in all the world there is no fairer than she.' Only Lanval was silent and did not praise her, remembering his own lady and how far she surpassed the Queen in beauty; and as he sat silent, his eyes turned from the Queen, he smiled a little at his thoughts.

The King was greatly pleased by the praise offered to the Queen, and did not dream that it was naught but flattery. Yet the Queen had marked how Lanval neither looked at her nor spoke her praise, and she had seen his little secret smile. Slighted and angry, she went to the King. 'Lord,' she said, 'of all your knights Sir Lanval alone finds me ugly and will not praise me. And he went against your wishes and did not even look at me.'

The King was angered and called Lanval to come to him. 'Why do you alone, of all my knights, speak no word in praise of the Queen?'

Lanval stood boldly before the King and answered him, 'Sir king, you do ill to make a mock of the Queen and set her up before us, inviting our lies and our flattery. For though she is fair enough, there could be very easily found a lady fairer than she.'

'Where, in all the world, would you find that fairer lady?' demanded the King.

'Sir king,' said Lanval quietly, 'my own lady is fairer by far than the Queen.'

The Queen cried out, 'Let him bring her here, that all men may choose between us.'

And after the King had frowned and thought on the matter, he said, 'Let it be as the Queen says. Fetch your lady and let us see her, and if she is accounted the fairer, then will I not hold your presumption against you. But if my queen is declared more lovely, then shall you be condemned for your insults to her.'

Sir Lanval mounted his horse and went at once to the river beyond the city; but when he came there, though he called on his lady over and over again, she never came to him, and he had no sight of her pavilion. 'It is because I have disobeyed her and spoken of our love,' he thought. And he rode back to the court, sick at heart.

'Since you have not brought your lady,' said the King, 'you shall lie in chains for a year. And if by this day twelve-month, your lady has not come, you shall be brought to judgement and condemned for slighting the Queen.'

So Lanval was cast into prison, in the dark and the cold; but always the worst of his torments was the thought that he had lost his lady for ever, because he had boasted of her.

When a year was passed and Whit Sunday was come again, Sir Lanval was brought before the King and his lords for judgement. 'Before you are sentenced, while there is yet time,' said the King, 'can you show us your lady today?'

Lanval bowed his head. 'Sir king, I cannot.'

'He has no lady, fair or otherwise,' mocked the Queen.

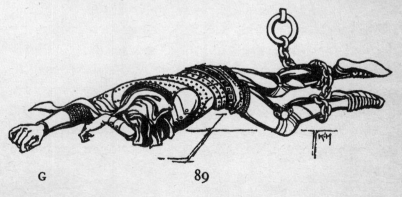

'Lords and knights,' said the King, 'what sentence shall we pass on him?'

The lords and the knights all debated the matter, and there were many who pitied Lanval, for he was much respected among them. And while they disputed, two damsels rode into the courtyard and asked to speak with the King. They were clothed in scarlet silk, and were both as lovely as the Queen herself. As they walked into the hall, a knight went to Sir Lanval where he stood in chains and said, 'Good friend, is one of these damsels your lady, come to save you?'

Lanval looked up at them. 'Neither is my lady. She is fairer by far.' And he sighed.

'Our mistress rides this way and asks that you will receive her,' said the damsels to the King.

'Willingly shall I welcome her, whoever she is,' replied the King. 'But first let us proceed with the judgement.'

Yet before the lords and knights could come to a decision, two other damsels rode into the courtyard and asked to speak with the King, and they were clothed in cloth of gold and rich embroidery.

The same knight who had spoken before went to Sir Lanval again. 'Is one of these damsels your lady? For in truth, both are most fair.'

But Lanval looked up and shook his head. 'Neither is my lady. She will not come to me.' And he wept.

'Our mistress rides this way and asks that you will receive her,' said the damsels to the King.

'Willingly shall I welcome her. Now let us proceed with the judgement, that it may be over and done with before she comes.' The King smiled with courtesy at the damsels, but the Queen bit her lip and frowned, for she saw how the two damsels were fairer than herself.

At that moment there came a noise from the streets of the city, a murmur of voices that filled the air. And through the streets, on a snow-white palfrey, rode a lady so beautiful that all the townspeople cried out in admiration. Into the courtyard of the castle she rode and asked to speak with the King.

As she came through the doorway into the great hall, three or more knights went to Sir Lanval. 'Here is a lady come, and there can be no lovelier in all the world. Surely she is your lady come to save you?'

And Lanval looked up and saw her as she walked towards the King, clothed all in white and purple and gold. 'I care not now how the judgement goes,' he whispered, 'nor what the sentence is. I care not whether I live or die, for I have seen her once more whom I thought never to see again.'

The lady from the fairy people stood before the King. 'I have loved your knight, Sir Lanval,' she said, 'and I would not see him come to harm because he has praised my beauty to the disparagement of your queen. Let all men judge between us now; and if she is thought more beautiful, then let him be condemned, but if I am considered the fairer, then let him go free.'

No man of them all, not even the King, could refrain from crying out that she was the more beautiful, and the Queen hid her face in her hands and ran from the hall. Then the King ordered that Sir Lanval should be freed from his chains and that his sword should be returned to him. And when it had been done, without a word or a glance for Lanval, the lady went from the hall, followed by her damsels. In the courtyard they mounted their palfreys and rode through the streets and out through the city gates and away across the fields to the river.

Lanval leapt upon a horse and rode after them, ever calling to his lady to stay for him. But no answer would she give. When she came to the bank of the river she and her damsels rode over, as though it had been dry land, and from the farther bank she looked back once. When she saw how Lanval would have urged his horse into the stream, she cried out, 'I am returning to my own land, and you may not come with me. Do not try to cross the river, or you will find only death.'

But Lanval dismounted from his terrified horse and leapt into the water. 'I would rather death than life without you,' he said.

The current caught him and swept him away, and the waters closed over his head, while his lady watched and seemed unmoved. But her damsels knelt at her feet and implored her pity, and she went to the water's edge and stretched out her hand to Sir Lanval and drew him out from the river half dead. When she held him in her arms and smiled at him, he opened his eyes; and when she kissed him, he rose up, alive and well. She bade him mount upon her white palfrey, and she set herself before him, and together they rode away to the fairy land whence she had come. And from that day no one ever saw Sir Lanval again.

The Werewolf

THERE dwelt in a castle in Brittany a young Baron who was much beloved of his King, and a good friend he was to him. This Baron had a wife, very fair and sweet to look upon, but quite otherwise in her heart, for though she smiled on her lord and spoke loving words, she cared not for him; all her heart was given to another knight, and she longed only that she might be rid of her lord and wedded to that other.

For three days out of every seven the Baron would be absent from his castle, and neither his lady nor any of his followers knew where he went or what he did during that time. The lady thought long on this and wondered how she might turn it to her advantage. One day, with many smiles and caresses, she said, 'There is a favour I would ask of you, dear lord.'

The Baron smiled. 'There is nothing I can deny you, as well you know,' he said.

'Then do not leave me for three days out of every week, for I am lonely when you are gone.'

The Baron turned away from her; he was no longer smiling and his voice was troubled. 'I would stay with you if I could. But alas, I cannot.'

'Tell me where you go,' she said. But he would not. Yet she coaxed and pleaded, weeping and protesting that he could not love her if he did not tell her; so that at last he could bear it no longer, and swearing her to secrecy, he said, 'Through no will of my own, I am a werewolf. Three days out of every seven must I spend as a wolf, running wild through the forest, a savage beast.'

'How does this change take place?' asked his lady.

'In the forest I put off my garments and lay them where I may find them again, and then I become a wolf. But when the three days are passed, I clothe myself and I am a man once more.'

Cunningly she asked, 'Dear lord, where do you hide your garments when you are become a wolf?'

'That, dearest, may I never tell to anyone, for if I could not find them when the three days were done, then I should have to remain as a wolf for ever, or until my garments were restored to me.'

Inwardly, she rejoiced when she heard this, and from that moment gave him no peace, forever asking him the same question and swearing that it was for his own good that she asked; and because he trusted her and believed her true, he told her at last. 'In the forest stands a ruined chapel, and near by, hidden by a bush, is a hollow stone. There do I hide my garments.'

The Werewolf

His lady kissed him and said she was proud to know how much he trusted her, and she swore his secret would come to no harm with her.

But the very next time that the Baron left his castle to go to the forest alone, she sent for the knight whom she loved and told him all. And she bade him go to the hollow stone by the ruined chapel and bring away her husband's garments. Greatly rejoicing, the knight did so, and she hid them in a coffer.

When the three days were passed, and the Baron in his wolf guise came to the hollow stone and found his garments gone, he knew his lady had betrayed him; but there was nothing that he might do to help himself, for if he but showed himself beyond the edge of the forest, men would loose hounds on him, and come against him with stones and cudgels, so that his life was likely to be quickly lost if he did not remain in the shelter of the trees.

When the weeks passed and the Baron did not come home, his lady wept a little and exclaimed a lot about the faithlessness of the lord who had abandoned her; and then she was married to the knight she loved, well pleased with the way things had gone.

But the wolf roamed in the forest, slaying and devouring after the manner of wolves, and ever grieving, until a year had passed, and one day the King chanced to hunt in that forest. The hounds came upon the tracks of the wolf and, baying and impatient, they followed him. All day the hounds trailed the wolf through the forest with the King and his courtiers close after them, and in the evening, the wolf, weary and torn by the thorns and the brambles, could go no farther, and he turned at bay, sure that his end had come. Then suddenly, beyond the ring of panting hounds, the bared fangs and the lolling tongues and the eager eyes, he saw the young King who had once been his friend. With his remaining strength he fought his way through the hounds, and running to the King, placed one paw upon the King's stirrup and laid his head upon the King's foot. Growling, the hounds came after him, but the King, much moved, beat them off and called to his companions to leash them.

'This poor wild creature has asked my mercy,' said the King. 'He shall have it. Let us go and leave him free in the forest.' And he turned and rode for his castle. Yet the wolf would not leave him, but limped along painfully beside his horse, even to the castle gates, so that all who saw marvelled at it. 'He has asked my protection,' said the King. 'He shall have it for so long as he pleases.' And he forbade anyone to harm the wolf and ordered fresh meat to be provided for him daily. And for his part, the wolf harmed no one in the castle, being ever gentle with everyone, and he followed the King like a dog; for had the courtiers not once been his companions in the jousting and on the tourney-ground, and had the King not been his friend? By day the wolf was always at the King's side, and at night he slept at the foot of his bed; and the King took more delight in his wolf than in any of his hounds.

Soon after, the King called all his vassals to court, and there he took counsel with them, and after, feasted them richly. Now, among those who were summoned was that same knight who had married the Baron's false lady, and when he and his followers came before the King, the wolf growled and leapt upon him, throwing him to the ground, and was restrained from doing him great hurt only with difficulty by those who stood around. The King was surprised, for until that moment the wolf had harmed no man. Yet it happened not once, but three times that he leapt upon the knight and was beaten off by the knight's friends; so that from fear that the knight or the wolf might be harmed, the King was forced to keep the wolf chained until the knight was gone from the castle, which he was glad to do as soon as he might, wondering much and not a little fearful.

It chanced, a few months later, that the King hunted again in the forest where he had found the wolf, and he lay for the night in a hunting-lodge on the edge of the forest close by the lands and the castle that had belonged to the Baron. The Baron's false lady, wishing to win favour for herself and her knight, rode in the morning from the castle, richly attended and bearing gifts for the King. But no sooner had she come into the presence of the King than the wolf gave a great howl and leapt at her throat, so that she cried out in fear. In an instant every man there save the King had drawn his dagger and hastened to defend the lady, and the wolf would surely have been slain, had the King not cried out to prevent it.

Then the King, holding the wolf close in his arms, so that he could neither be harmed nor do harm, said slowly, 'This is the lady who was wife to that baron who was once my friend and who went no man knows where. And the knight whom my wolf attacked, he is the second lord of this lady and now rules the lands which were once my friend's.' And he ordered the lady and her knight to be bound, and they were locked away in a dungeon. And there in the cold and the darkness, with little to drink and less to eat, the lady in her terror confessed her crime and told where she had hidden the Baron's garments.

Immediately the king sent for them, and when they were brought, he laid them before the wolf, while all watched to see what might happen. But the wolf looked at the garments and made no move.

'He is no more than a wolf,' said the courtiers. 'The good Baron is lost to us for ever.'

But the King said gently, 'It would be a great shame to a knight to turn from a wolf to a man before the eyes of so many.' And he rose and took up the garments and went to his own bedchamber with the wolf following him, and he laid the garments on the bed and came out from the room alone, locking the door behind him. After a little while he called two others and they went together to the bedchamber. The King unlocked the door and they entered, and there on the King's bed lay the Baron, asleep. And no man could have been happier than the King in that moment.

The false lady and her knight were driven forth from the kingdom, and the Baron regained his castle and his lands. But most of his time he spent, whether as a wolf or as a man, at the court of the King.

LEGENDS FROM
THE FRENCH PROVINCES

Mélusine

IN the county of Poitou there once lived a young
knight named Raymond. He was a younger brother
of the Count of Forez, and cousin to the Count of
Poitiers.

One day, when he was at the court of his cousin, while
out hunting in the forest of Coulombiers, he became
separated from his companions and wandered on alone,
seeking a path that would lead him back to his cousin's
castle. But darkness fell before he had found a way.

Suddenly, in a wide forest clearing, he saw the glint
of moonlight upon water; and his horse being tired and
thirsty, he rode towards the little spring which gushed out
from a rock, gleaming like silver with pale woodland
flowers growing all about it. While his horse drank gratefully from the cool water, Raymond looked about him,
and was aware of a lovely maiden who sat beside the
rock. He stared at her in surprise, and saw in the bright

moonlight how she smiled at him. 'Who are you, most beautiful lady?' he asked.

'I am Mélusine,' she said, rising and coming to him.

He was so astounded by her beauty that he could only stare at her; and after a time he said, 'I am but a poor knight, a younger brother of the lord of Forez, yet had I lands and riches of my own, I would ask you to be my bride.'

'I know who you are,' said Mélusine, 'and I know also that your cousin the Count of Poitiers loves you well. If you were to ask him, he would grant you land. Go to him, ask him for this spring and as much of the land about it as may be covered by the skin of a deer. Then return and speak with me again.'

Like a man in a dream, Raymond rode on through the forest, and it was almost dawn and he was on the road to Poitiers and in sight of the castle walls, before he realized how strange her commands had been. 'The land covered by the skin of even the largest deer will be a very little land,' he thought.

But he did not for a moment consider acting other than as she had bidden him, and he went to the Count of Poitiers and said, 'As you know, lord, I have few possessions of my own. I beg that you will grant me a little land in your forest of Coulombiers. No more than a spring which flows in a clearing, and as much land about it as may be covered by the hide of a deer.'

'Cousin,' replied the Count, 'I would give you more than that.'

'It is all I ask,' said Raymond.

'Then it is yours,' said the Count.

Raymond rode back to the spring in the forest, followed by his servants, and they carried with them the hide of a large deer. By the spring Mélusine awaited him. 'You have done as I bade you?' she asked.

'It is done, and the land has been granted me.'

Then Mélusine set the servants to cutting the deer-hide into the thinnest strips, and these thongs she had them knot together until they had fashioned a long cord. When this cord was laid end to end about the spring, it enclosed a wide stretch of land, so that Raymond saw how he was no longer a poor, landless knight.

'Now I may ask you to marry me,' he said joyfully to Mélusine.

'I will marry you,' she answered, 'but it must be on one condition. Swear that never will you try to see me on any Saturday in any week, or ask what I do on that day.'

'I swear it,' said Raymond. 'And may I lose you for ever if I do not keep my word.'

Now, Mélusine was a fairy woman, and she was doomed, on the Saturday of each week, to change into a serpent from her waist down to her toes. So long as no one saw her when she was half-woman and half-serpent, she might live as happily and die as peacefully as any mortal woman; but if she were once seen, then it was decreed that she would have to keep her serpent shape for ever, and with it, gain immortality.

Raymond married Mélusine, and she built for him by her enchantments, with no more than a mouthful of water and three armfuls of stones, a great castle on his land and named it Lusignan; and there they lived in great happiness for many years. And never once in all that time did Raymond question her as to what she did on Saturdays, nor try to see her on that day.

Ten sons were born to Mélusine and Raymond, and each one of them was strange and wonderful, differing, through his fairy blood, from other boys. Gui, the eldest, had one eye green and the other red; Odo had one ear that was large and one ear that was small, and his hearing was very sharp; Urian was crooked-eyed, and Antoine was marked with a lion's paw upon his cheek; Regnault had but one eye, yet with it he could see for more than fifty miles; Geoffroi had tusks like a wild boar, and more than a wild boar's courage; Froimond would have been considered most handsome, had he not had a mole on his nose; the skin of Raymond, who was named after his father, was as black as soot, and Thierri had fur like a bear; whilst the very youngest son had three eyes. But for all their strange appearance, these sons of Mélusine and Raymond grew up to do great deeds and to win great riches for themselves and to be much respected.

Raymond's eldest brother, the Count of Forez, envied Raymond his castle of Lusignan and his beautiful wife, and he never saw either without wondering how he might destroy his brother's happiness, which was greater than his own.

One day when the Count of Forez came to Lusignan with his followers, Raymond, as was his wont, received him with unfeigned joy and great hospitality, because he was truly fond of his brother and had no knowledge of his envy. But, since it was a Saturday, Mélusine was not present.

'Where is my fair sister?' asked the Count. And Raymond could give him no answer save, 'I do not see her on Saturdays.'

Immediately the Count saw his chance. 'That is indeed strange,' he said. 'What is the reason for it?'

'It is as Mélusine wishes,' replied Raymond.

'Have you never wondered what she does on Saturdays?' asked the Count cunningly. 'Have you never wondered why her sons are not as the sons of other women? Have  you never considered that Mélusine might be a witch or an evil spirit?'

'Mélusine is good and beautiful, and she is my beloved wife,' said Raymond. But his brother's words had sown a dreadful doubt in his heart, and for a long time after, he was silent, wondering. At last the Count said, 'You would do well to be sure of that, my brother, before you trust her further. The day may come when she will do you great harm.'

Tormented by his doubts and urged by his brother,

Raymond went to the tower where Mélusine hid herself on Saturdays. The door of the tower was locked, but he looked through the keyhole, and there in the room in the tower he saw Mélusine combing her hair. Down to her waist she was the wife he knew and loved, but the rest of her was the body and the tail of a serpent, covered with blue and silver scales. Appalled at the sight, Raymond cried out, and Mélusine, hearing him, gave one wild shriek and vanished through the window of the tower room, and Raymond never saw her again.

In time Raymond died and was succeeded by Geoffroi of the boar's tusks, the bravest of all his sons. But Mélusine, immortal in her serpent shape, though invisible to all, never forgot the line which she and Raymond had founded; and always, whenever danger threatened the house of Lusignan, or a lord of Lusignan lay dying, Mélusine's wild crying would be heard all around the castle, above the wind.

The Korrigan

IN the waters of each ivied, moss-covered fountain of Brittany, lived a korrigan, who, it was said, had once built that fountain for herself. In the old days the country women with their wide, stiff head-dresses would come to fetch water from these fountains in their earthenware pitchers or brass pots, and they would linger awhile to gossip and chat with a neighbour, secure from the spite of the korrigan by reason of the crucifix or the statue of the Blessed Virgin which had been placed upon the stonework of the fountain to curb the fairy being's power. For without the protection of these Christian figures, no village wife could be sure that beside the fountain she might not meet the korrigan herself, in the likeness of an old, old woman, her face as wrinkled as last year's apple and her red eyes bright with malice. But once the fountain had been guarded by an image of the Saviour or His Mother, the korrigan would no longer be seen there by day; though at night she would still appear, sitting beside the water in her own shape, fair and lovely, combing her long yellow hair, with the fountain as her mirror.

The korrigans were skilled in healing and would give charms to those who respected their powers and showed them honour. But it was always held unwise to vex them: to throw stones into their fountains, or to spy upon them by night; and most of all, one had to beware of them upon a Saturday, for Saturday being dedicated to the Blessed Virgin, the korrigans were then at their most spiteful.

Some peasants believed the korrigans to be the spirits of the Druid priestesses who once lived in Brittany and served the old gods; but others believed them to be the souls of those Celtic princesses, who, when the Christian faith was first brought to Brittany, rejected it, and so were cursed to the end of time. But however that may be, the korrigans have always hated Christian priests above all other men, and they have ever been eager to find mortal husbands and to steal away mortal children, and many are the stories the Bretons tell of them. Here is one of these tales.

Once, on a summer's day, a farmer's wife left her few-months-old child in his cradle close by the open farmhouse door while she went down to the fields to speak with her husband. Before she left, she kissed him and smoothed the coverlet, but she forgot to make the sign of the cross over him to keep him from harm. She was gone but a short time, yet while she was gone a korrigan came by, and looking in through the door, saw the child in the cradle. The babe's fair hair, like ripened grain, his blue eyes like cornflowers, and his contented smile were more than she could resist; and quickly she snatched the child from his cradle and was away to her fountain, leaving in his place her own ugly little poulpican, or dwarf, wrinkled and hideous, with sharp eyes and spiteful glance.

Such was the strength of the korrigan's enchantment, that at first the mother noticed nothing wrong with the child she supposed her own, though she wondered why her babe, formerly so smiling and contented, should have of a sudden become so fretful and perverse. But as time went on she saw the change both in the appearance and the behaviour of the child, and was disturbed by the wilful, peevish temper, and strangely frightened by the intent, malicious stare of the dark eyes.

Every now and then she would speak to her husband of it, but the farmer would only say, in his easy-going fashion, with a shrug of his shoulders, 'A child changes as it grows older. The child becomes a boy, and the boy becomes a man. Nothing stays the same for ever.'

But her disquiet remained, and as the years passed, it increased. As indeed well it might, for the poulpican grew slowly in body but fast in wits, and a more sly, cunning, and spiteful child it would have been hard to find for many miles around. Yet when the mother, with tears, told his misdeeds to her husband, the farmer only said, 'All boys are mischievous. I was myself. He will grow out of it.'

But the poulpican became worse instead of better. He played his tricks on the men who worked for the farmer, he tormented the animals, and he gave the farmer's wife no peace with his wicked ways. When at last he was old enough, he was sent out to the fields to watch the cows. 'It will keep him out of mischief,' said the farmer. But he tied furze branches to the tails of all the cows, so that when they tried to flick the flies away, they pricked themselves with the thorns and were driven almost wild, while the poulpican laughed and screeched with glee at the sight.

One stormy day, a neighbour, riding home from market with a calf which he had bought, knocked on the farm-house door with a message for the farmer. He was wearing his thick cloak against the rain, and he carried the calf before him, slung across the horse's neck. The poulpican looked out of the window at his knock and saw what resembled a three-headed beast, wrapped in a cloak. 'I saw the egg before I saw the white hen,' he cried out, 'and I saw the acorn before I saw the oak-tree. But never did I see such a sight as this.'

The neighbour was puzzled at hearing such words from a ten-year-old child, and he repeated them to the farmer's wife. Distressed and suspicious, she determined to test her supposed son. One evening, when he was in the kitchen, she took the shell of an egg, filling it with flour and oatmeal and sprinkling it with salt and pepper and stirring the mixture round with a tiny spoon. The poulpican watched her. 'What are you doing, mother?' he asked.

'Preparing supper for your father's men,' she replied.

'Preparing supper for ten men in one eggshell, mother?'

'Yes, my child.'

The poulpican stared at her. 'I saw the egg before I saw the white hen,' he said, 'and I saw the acorn before I saw the oak-tree. But never did I see such a sight as this.'

The farmer's wife now felt sure that there was something very strange about the child, and she watched him carefully; and for his part, as though he guessed, he watched her also, with the intentness of a creature much more than ten years old, and with a spite that seemed to grow more evil every day.

One evening she told her fears to her husband. 'I am afraid of him,' she whispered. 'Husband, he is no child of ours.'

And finally even the farmer was forced to admit that she was right. 'He is no doubt some fairy creature who means us no good,' he said.

His wife sobbed and wrung her hands. 'He will do us some great harm before very long, I am sure of that. If only we might be rid of him.'

They talked of the matter long into the night, sitting beside the dying fire, and at last they decided that they must kill the poulpican before he brought disaster upon them or upon their men. 'I will do it quickly, while he sleeps,' said the farmer. He took up a knife and sharpened it, and went to where the poulpican lay sleeping. But before the farmer had reached him, the poulpican was awake and had guessed his intention, and he leapt up with one wild scream.

Away beside her fountain, the korrigan heard his cry and came at once. The farmhouse door flew open, and there in the doorway the terrified farmer and his wife saw the korrigan holding by the hand a tall, ten-year-old boy, with hair like ripened grain and eyes like blue cornflowers. She thrust him towards them. 'Take your child,' she said, 'and give me back my own.'

The poulpican ran to her, and she took him in her arms and was gone; and laughing and crying all at once, the farmer and his wife embraced their son.

The Stones of Plouhinec

IN parts of Brittany are found groups of the great stones known as menhirs, arranged in circles or in avenues, like tall, rough-hewn pillars. Country people will tell you that long ago they were set up by the kerions, the fairy dwarfs, and that beneath many of them the kerions hid their gold and treasure. Each group of menhirs has its own legend, and this is the story of the Stones of Plouhinec.

Near the little town of Plouhinec, close by the Breton coast, there lies a barren stretch of moor where only coarse grass grows, and the yellow broom of Brittany. On this plain stand the stones of Plouhinec, two long rows of them.

On the edge of the moor there once lived a farmer with his sister Rozennik. Rozennik was young and pretty, and she had many suitors from Plouhinec, yet she saved her smiles for Bernèz, a poor lad who worked on her brother's farm; but the farmer refused to consider Bernèz as a suitor until he could show him his pockets full of gold.

One Christmas Eve, while the farmer was feasting his men in the farmhouse kitchen, as was his yearly custom, there came a knock on the door, and outside in the cold wind stood an old beggar who asked for a meal and shelter for the night. He looked a sly, artful old rogue, and one whom it would have been unwise to trust, but because it was Christmas Eve, he was made welcome and given a bowl of soup and a place by the fire. After supper the farmer took him out to the stable and said that he might sleep there, on a pile of straw. In the stable were the ox who drew the farmer's plough and the donkey who carried to market whatever the farmer had to sell.

The beggar was just falling asleep when midnight struck, and, as everyone knows, at midnight on Christmas Eve all the beasts in a stable can speak to each other, in memory of that first Christmas in the stable at Bethlehem.

'It is a cold night,' said the donkey.

As soon as the old beggar heard the donkey speak, he pretended to be asleep and snoring, but he kept very wide awake, for it was a habit with him, whenever he could, to listen to other people talking, in case he heard something to his advantage, or else something to their disadvantage, which he might put to profitable purpose.

'No colder,' replied the ox, 'than it will be on New Year's Eve when the stones of Plouhinec go down to the river to drink and leave their treasure uncovered. Only once in every hundred years that comes to pass.' The ox looked down at the beggar, snoring on the straw. 'If this old man knew what we know, he would be off, seven nights from now, to fill his pockets from the kerions' hoard.'

114

'Small good would it do him,' said the donkey, 'unless he carried with him a bunch of crowsfoot and a five-leaved trefoil. Without those plants in his hand, the stones would crush him when they returned.'

'Even the crowsfoot and the five-leaved trefoil would not be enough,' said the ox, 'for, remember, whoever takes the treasure of the stones must offer in exchange a Christian soul, or the stolen treasure will turn to dust. And though a man may easily find crowsfoot, and he may, if he searches long enough, find a five-leaved trefoil, where will he find a Christian man willing to die for him?'

'That is true enough,' agreed the donkey; and the two beasts went on to talk of other matters.

But the old beggar had heard enough to make him determined to steal the treasure, and he was up and away from the farm at the first light of day, and for six days he searched all about the countryside for crowsfoot and tre-foil. He found the crowsfoot soon enough, and he found trefoil, but none with more than three leaves; until on the very last day but one of the old year, he found a five-leaved trefoil. Eagerly he hurried back to Plouhinec, reaching the town on the next morning, and went at once to the moor, that he might spy out a spot to hide himself as near to the stones as possible, to be close at hand when they went, at midnight, down to the river.

But he found someone there before him. Young Bernèz had brought his midday meal of bread and cheese to eat sitting alone beneath the largest of the stones whilst he dreamt of Rozennik, and having finished his meal, he was spending the few spare minutes that remained to him before he had to return to work in idly carving a cross upon the stone by which he sat.

'What are you doing?' asked the old beggar, who recognized him as one of the men from the farmhouse where he had spent Christmas Eve.

Bernèz smiled. 'This holy sign may be of help or comfort to someone, one day. It is as good a way as any of passing an idle moment, to carve a cross on a stone.'

'That is so,' replied the beggar; but while he was speaking he was remembering the look in Bernèz' eyes as he had watched Rozennik at the feasting on Christmas Eve, for his own sharp eyes missed little, and a cunning thought came into his head. 'What would you do,' he asked, 'if you had your pockets full of gold?'

'Why,' said Bernèz, 'that is easy. I would go to the farmer and ask for Rozennik for my wife. He would not refuse me then, and I think that she would not say no to me.'

The beggar looked about him and leant his head close to Bernèz. 'I can tell you how to fill your pockets with gold, and a sack or two besides.'

'How?' asked Bernèz, surprised.

And the beggar told him what he had learnt from the ox and the ass; all save how a bunch of crowsfoot and a five-leaved trefoil were necessary if one was not to be crushed by the stones as they returned from the river, and how a Christian soul must be offered in exchange for the gold. When he had finished, Bernèz' eyes shone and he clasped the old man's hand. 'You are a good friend indeed, to tell me this and to share your good fortune with me. I will meet you here before midnight.' He finished carving his cross joyfully, and ran back to his work on the farm; whilst the beggar chuckled to himself at the thought of how easily he had found someone to die in exchange for the gold.

Before midnight they were waiting together, Bernèz and the old beggar, hidden behind a clump of broom in the darkness. No sooner had midnight struck than there was a noise as of a great thundering, the ground shook, and the huge stones heaved themselves out of the earth and began to move down to the river. 'Now,' said the beggar, 'this is the moment.' They ran forward and looked down into the pits where the stones had stood, and there, at the bottom of each pit was a heap of treasure. The beggar opened the sacks he had brought with him and began to fill them hastily, one after the other; but Bernèz, his heart full of the thought of Rozennik, filled only his pockets with the gold.

It seemed no more than a moment later that the earth began to tremble again and the ground echoed as though to the tramp of a giant army marching. The stones, having drunk from the river, were returning to their places. Bernèz cried out in horror as he saw them loom out of the darkness. 'Quickly, quickly, or we shall be crushed to death.' But the old beggar laughed and held up his bunch of crowsfoot and his five-leaved trefoil. 'Not I,' he said, 'for I have these magic plants to protect me. But you, you are lost, and it is as well for me, since unless a Christian soul is given in exchange, my treasure will crumble away in the morning.'

With terror Bernèz heard him and saw that he had

spoken the truth, for the first of the stones moved aside
when it reached the beggar and his magic herbs, and after
it the other stones passed on either side of him, leaving
him untouched, to move close together again as they came
near to Bernèz.

The young man was too afraid to try to escape. He
covered his face with his hands and waited when he saw the
largest stone of all bear down on him. But above the very
spot where Bernèz crouched, trembling, the stone paused,
and remained there, towering over him as though to protect him, while all the other stones had to move aside and
so pass him by. And when Bernèz, amazed, dared to look
up, he saw that the stone which sheltered him was the one
upon which he had carved a cross.

Not until all the other stones were in their places did it
move, and then it went by Bernèz and on to where its own

pit showed dark, with the shining treasure at the bottom. On its way it overtook the beggar, stumbling along with his heavy sacks of gold. He heard it come after him and held out the bunch of crowsfoot and the five-leaved trefoil with a triumphant shout. But because of the cross carved upon it, the magic herbs had no longer any power over the stone and it went blindly on its way, crushing the old beggar beneath it. And so it passed on to its own place and settled into the earth again until another hundred years should have gone by. But Bernèz ran back home to the farm, as fast as his legs could carry him; and when, in the morning, he showed his pockets full of gold, the farmer did not refuse to give him his sister. And as for Rozennik, she did not say no, for she would have had him anyway, had the choice rested with her.

Pierre of Provence

THERE were in the old days a Count of Provence and his lady who had an only son named Pierre. Pierre was a handsome, courteous youth, a great joy and blessing to his parents. When he had been made a knight, he took part in the tournaments and the jousting, and it was soon seen that in all Provence he had not his equal. One day he heard of the beauty of Magdelona, the daughter of the King of Naples, in Italy, and he determined to journey to Naples to see her for himself. His parents were sad at his going, yet they did not seek to keep him with them, but only bade him return to them before a year was passed; and this Pierre promised.

Gaily and eagerly young Pierre rode into Italy from France, following the coast-line of the blue Mediterranean. When he came to Naples, he found all the city holding festival, for the King had decreed a tournament in honour of the birthday of the Princess. Pierre entered the lists with the finest knights of Naples, but he easily had the better of them all, and was proclaimed the winner. The King himself gave him the prize he had so well deserved, and as Pierre took it from his hands, he saw the Princess Magdelona seated beside her father, and he knew that the reports of her had not lied. Indeed, he found her far more beautiful than he had hoped, and instantly he loved her and vowed to have no other lady. And the Princess, for her part, lost her own heart to the young knight from France; but she told no one of this save her old nurse.

Now, the Princess's nurse longed more than anything to see her mistress happy, and she cared nothing that Pierre was no more than the son of a count, so long as the Princess loved him, and she soon contrived that Pierre and Magdelona should meet secretly. They told their love to each other and swore faith for evermore, and Pierre gave Magdelona a ring which had been his mother's, and she gave him a golden chain. After that, though they met but seldom, the old nurse would often carry messages of love between them.

When it lacked but a few weeks to the time when he would have been from his home for a full year, Pierre remembered his promise to his parents, and sought a means to speak with Magdelona that he might bid her farewell until he could return to Naples once again. With the aid of the nurse they met one evening. 'I have to leave you, dearest, but I will return to you,' said Pierre, and he told her of his promise.

Magdelona wept and begged him not to go. 'Each day,'

she said, 'suitors come to my father to ask for my hand, the sons of kings and kings themselves. Sooner or later he will consider one of them worthy of me, and by the time that you return I may be married to another and gone to a distant land.'

'I am only the son of a count,' said Pierre. 'How could I dream that your father would give me your hand, when he has refused so many princes?'

'We shall not ask his consent,' said Magdelona. 'Take me with you, Pierre. Take me with you and let us go from Naples this very night.'

So, secretly and unseen of any, Pierre and Magdelona rode through the gates of Naples in the dark, and by dawn they had gone many miles. But by that time Magdelona was too tired to ride any farther, so at the edge of a wood near the seashore, they dismounted to rest. Wrapped in her mantle and with Pierre's cloak for a pillow, the Princess lay down and was at once asleep, while Pierre sat beside her to watch over her.

As she slept, a little casket of carved wood slipped from her hands and fell upon the grass. Pierre took it up, and with loving curiosity wondered what alone out of all her treasures it was that she had chosen to bring with her, and he opened the casket and saw inside the ring that he had given her. Touched and happy at her devotion to his gift, he laid the casket, still open, at her side. Then he fell to thinking of the joyous homecoming that awaited him in his own land of Provence, and of the kindness with which his parents would greet his lovely bride; and even as he was counting how many days must pass before they would have reached Provence and safety, a raven, attracted by the glittering of the ring, swooped down with a hoarse croak, and seizing the little casket in its beak, flew off towards the sea.

Pierre leapt to his feet, and seeing that the bird had alighted on a rock near the water's edge, he ran towards it. But the raven espied his coming, and spreading its black wings, it flew away out across the sea. Dismayed, Pierre stood on the shore and watched, and then he saw how the raven, tired by the weight of the casket, dropped it, so that it floated on the waves.

Drawn up on the beach lay an old boat, left there by some fisherman. Pierre dragged it to the water and pushed out from the shore, rowing with all his might for the spot where the casket floated. With the help of a wind from the land, he reached it safely and snatched it thankfully from the waves, only to find that the ring was gone. Sadly he thought, 'It is lost for ever at the bottom of the sea, and I must return to Magdelona without it.' But when he would have rowed again for the shore, he found the wind so strongly against him that he had a hard struggle to fight towards land, and as he rowed, the oars, which were old and brittle, snapped, and the little boat was blown far out to sea, where it drifted helplessly. Despairing, not for himself, though he feared he would surely be drowned, but for the Princess, Pierre prayed that Magdelona might come to no harm alone.

After a day and a night adrift at sea, Pierre sighted a ship which flew the crescent flag of the Saracens. When she came close, her captain ordered a boat to be lowered that

Pierre might be fetched on board. When he saw Pierre's youth and his noble bearing, and the rich gold chain which he wore about his neck, the captain reckoned him a man of note and one who would fetch a good price, and he treated him fittingly. When the ship reached harbour in Alexandria, Pierre was sold for a slave to the sultan of that city.

The sultan was a kindly man, and seeing how Pierre served him honestly, he made him, though a Christian, a high official in his household. But Pierre, for all the favour that was shown to him, was ever grieving for Magdelona and his parents, whom he believed he would never see again. One day, however, he had the good fortune to discover a plot against the sultan's life, and in reward for his loyalty, the sultan gave him his freedom and many gifts, and at once Pierre set sail for France.

In Italy, meanwhile, when the Princess awoke on the edge of the wood by the seashore and found herself alone and the casket which held the ring gone, she called and called to Pierre and searched all about for him; but when he gave no answer and she discovered no trace of him, it seemed as though he had deserted her. But this she could not believe. Then she saw their two horses, still tethered where he had left them. 'If he had wearied of my company and ceased to love me, or if he had feared my father's wrath too much to take me home with him, then he would have ridden away and not left his horse,' she thought. And though she was glad that Pierre had not deserted her, she was fearful that some dreadful fate must have overtaken him. She was afraid, too, that soon her father's men would be searching throughout Naples for her, and that, unaccompanied, in her rich garments, she would be easily found and taken back to the palace to face both her father's anger and marriage with one of her many suitors. 'If I may not be Pierre's bride,' she said to herself, 'then I will be the bride of no other man.' She freed the horses and watched them trot away, then she set off alone on foot along the road from Naples.

After a short time she met a peasant woman wearing a gown of grey homespun cloth and a brown mantle and hood. 'Good friend,' said Magdelona, 'I pray you, change clothes with me.' The woman stared at her as though she could not believe her ears, but when she found that Magdelona was not jesting, she hastily did as she was asked, and the Princess, wearing the grey gown with her jewels hidden beneath it, and with the brown hood pulled well over her head, left her admiring herself at the roadside.

Magdelona, begging her way as she went, came at last to Rome, and there she sought refuge in a hospice for poor pilgrims to that city, and in this place she helped the good nuns to care for them. But one day, in the church of St Peter, where she had gone to pray for Pierre, she saw her uncle, the Duke of Calabria, and she feared that her father had sent him to Rome in search of her. She determined to leave the city at once, and while she was wondering where she might go, it came into her mind to see the land where Pierre had been born; and taking with her the jewels which she still had, in the company of some pilgrims who were returning from Rome to their own land of France, she journeyed to Provence.

At the mouth of the River Rhône, in the little town of

Aigues-Mortes, built upon a salt marsh where the red flamingoes nested, she lodged in the house of a kindly widow. She asked this widow for news of the Count of Provence. 'Alas,' said the old woman, 'these are sad days for our Count and his lady. Their only son has been gone from them these two years, and they fear that he is dead.' Magdelona wept at her words, and determined to spend the remainder of her days in Provence, so that if by any chance Pierre were still living and returned to his home, she would be there to hear of it.

She sold her jewels, and on one of the many little islets in the mouth of the harbour at Aigues-Mortes she built a hospice for poor sailors and fishermen, calling it the Hospice of St Peter, in remembrance of Pierre; and there she spent all her days for five years and more, in works of charity and caring for the sick, helped by several good women of the town.

In time the fame of her hospice reached the ears of the Count, and one day the Countess herself came to the little island. At the sight of Pierre's mother, Magdelona wept. 'Why do you weep?' asked the Countess.

'I weep,' replied Magdelona, 'because you have lost your son.'

'Your pity must indeed be great, if you can weep for one who was a stranger,' said the Countess.

'He was no stranger,' said Magdelona; and she told the Countess her whole story. 'Yet I beg of you,' she ended, 'that you will keep my secret, for I would not return to Naples. Rather would I end my days in the land which Pierre promised would be my home.'

The Countess kissed her. 'You may trust me and my lord as you trusted Pierre. And there will always be an honoured place for you in our castle, for you should have been our daughter.'

But Magdelona preferred to remain in her hospice, tending the sick, and she asked only that the Countess would visit her often, that they might talk together of Pierre.

One day, the Count's cook, on cutting open a large fish, found inside it a golden ring. Full of wonder, he took the ring to his master, and instantly the Countess set eyes on it, she knew it for the ring which she had once given Pierre. This seemed to her proof that Pierre had been drowned and was indeed dead, and full of sorrow she went to Magdelona and showed her the ring. 'It was the ring he gave to me,' said Magdelona weeping. 'But maybe heaven will be kind to us and bring him safely home, even yet.'

A few months later, some fishermen knocked at night on the door of the Hospice of St Peter, bringing with them a shipwrecked man whom they had found, all but dead, on the shore. Magdelona knew him at once. It was Pierre. The ship he had sailed on from Alexandria had been wrecked within sight of the coast of France, and he alone had escaped from the sea.

Devotedly she tended him and prayed for him, never leaving his side, and one day Pierre opened his eyes and saw her and feebly stretched out a hand to her. 'Magdelona, is it indeed you, or am I dreaming?'

'It is I,' she said, 'and you are wide awake.' As soon as she knew that Pierre would live, she sent word to the Count and the Countess, and they hastened to the hospice.

Their joy at finding their beloved son once more was beyond all words.

And soon, with great rejoicing, Pierre was married to Magdelona, and she left the hospice in the hands of the good women who had helped her there, and went to live at the castle.

In time, the King of Naples, who had never ceased sending forth men to search for his daughter, learnt from one of them who had travelled disguised to Provence, where she was. In his great happiness at knowing that she was not dead, he forgave her and Pierre; and since he had no other child, at his death, his kingdom fell to Pierre; and thus, for some years, the county of Provence was united with the kingdom of Naples.

The Cliff of the Two Lovers

IN Normandy, near where the River Andelle flows into the Seine, there stands a high chalk cliff known as *La Côte des Deux Amants*: the Cliff of the Two Lovers. In the Middle Ages this cliff lay in the lands of a certain count. The Count was brave in war and a fierce warrior, but he was a harsh and cruel man and much feared by all who served him. He had one daughter, Calixte, who could not have been less like her father, being gentle and kindly to all. She was, moreover, very fair to look upon, a great joy to all who beheld her.

The Count had in his service a young squire named Edmond, of an age with Calixte. Edmond came of a poor family and was not of noble birth, yet he hoped in time, through his skill at arms and by an honourable life, to be accounted worthy of knighthood. He had spent his childhood and his boyhood in the castle of the Count, and had been the constant playfellow of Calixte, and to each other they were as brother and sister rather than count's daughter and poor squire.

One day, when Calixte and Edmond were some seventeen years old, the Count and all his following rode out to hunt a boar which had been seen in the forest. With them, at her father's bidding, rode Calixte, lovelier than ever, her flaxen hair so long that it hung down her back as far as the tail of her white palfrey, so that with the sunlight turning the silver into gold, one might not tell where the one ended and the other began.

Calixte cared little for hunting, since her soft heart had no liking to see the wild creatures slain, but it was a fine morning, and all about her in the forest the birds sang, and there were flowers everywhere to delight her eyes. Before long she had fallen a distance behind the others, so much preferring the beauty about her to the thrill of the chase, and no one missed her save Edmond, who also hung back a little that he might be near Calixte, should any danger threaten her, alone in the forest.

Suddenly, through the trees, there came to Calixte the triumphant notes of the horns, proclaiming that the boar had been sighted and roused. It reminded her that it were best she should be with the others before her father missed her, for he would wish her to be there for the kill. With a sigh, she urged her horse to a canter, making for where the sounds of the hunt were loudest: the baying of the hounds and the shouts of the huntsmen. But the white palfrey stumbled over the root of a tree, too well hidden by ferns and moss, and Calixte was thrown to the ground. She lay there for a moment and then sat up, shaken and wondering if the pain in her foot meant that she would not be able to stand to remount her horse unaided.

The cry of the hounds came nearer and nearer, and just as she was about to try to rise, there was a plunging through the undergrowth and the huge boar broke cover only a few yards away. Calixte gave a cry of fear. The boar stared about it, its little eyes gleaming red and angry, and saw Calixte. Furiously, it made ready to charge. 'Dear God,' prayed Calixte, 'help me, for I am as good as dead.' In that very moment a figure sprang from the bushes and stood between her and the maddened boar: Edmond, who had heard her cry out. He dropped to one knee and held his hunting spear ready to meet the boar's charge, and in an instant it was upon him and Calixte closed her eyes in terror. But in its rush the boar was impaled on Edmond's spear. Quickly he rose, and before it could recover, he had driven the spear through its heart.

He turned and ran to Calixte, kneeling on the grass beside her, his face white with anxiety. He took her in his arms. 'Calixte, dearest, are you hurt?' In his voice was the terror of a youth for the maiden whom he loves, not the concern of a brother for his sister.

She clung to him. 'Edmond, you might have been killed for my sake. How very brave you are.' In her voice was the pride of a lady in the deeds of her knight, and not sisterly affection. For a moment they looked into each other's eyes, reading each other's thoughts, and then they kissed.

Edmond helped her to her feet, and then the hunt with the Count at its head came upon them. At once the Count and all with him saw the boar lying dead, transfixed by Edmond's spear, and Calixte, pale and trembling, about to remount her horse, and they knew how Edmond must have saved her life. The Count dismounted and went to them. He embraced Edmond. 'Good squire,' he said, 'you have saved my daughter's life, no reward can be too great for you. Ask of me what you will, and it shall be yours.'

At first Edmond was silent, then he stole a glance at Calixte. He looked back at the Count and spoke boldly but quietly. 'There is no reward that I would ask of you, lord, save that you would give me your daughter for my wife.'

For a minute or more the Count stared at Edmond as though he did not believe what he had heard. When at last he answered, his hard voice was even harder than its wont. 'You, no more than a squire, dare to ask for that?' His eyes blazed in anger and he clenched his fists. 'My daughter shall marry a nobleman, a knight who has proved his strength and his courage. She shall be the bride of one her equal in birth. Do you think that I should give her to a low-born knave like you?'

Edmond's voice when he answered was hardly more than a whisper, but he kept it steady and he did not show his fear of the Count. 'I have served you well and faithfully, and you have been pleased to praise me, now and then. I hoped that one day I might be considered worthy to receive knighthood at your hands. And though I am, as you say, not of noble birth, I think my honour is no less than any lord's.'

The Count stepped forward, as though he would have

struck Edmond; and then he paused and looked at him, young and slim and little taller than Calixte, and suddenly he laughed. And at the sound of his laugh his followers grew pale, for they had learnt to fear a certain laugh of his more than his voice raised in anger. 'My daughter,' said the Count, 'to wed with a lad like you!' He laughed again. 'Edmond, do you know that cliff which lies between the Ardelle and the Seine?'

'Indeed, lord, I do.' Edmond was puzzled and suspicious, but he gave no sign of it.

The Count smiled. 'Tomorrow,' he said, 'you shall climb that cliff, carrying Calixte upon your back. If you can reach the top without once pausing to take breath or rest, I shall consider you a man indeed, one well worthy of knighthood and a fitting bridegroom for my daughter.' His smile mocked Edmond. 'Come, how say you, will you try your strength and climb?'

Edmond met his scorn, unfaltering. 'I will climb the cliff,' he said. And standing beside him, Calixte, unseen, slipped her hand in one of his and held it very tightly.

'Tomorrow then,' said the Count, 'be ready to win knighthood and your bride.' He turned away as though he cared no more for the matter; as indeed he did not, for he was certain that Edmond would fail and be made a mockery in the sight of all, and not least in the sight of Calixte.

A man was sent to set at the very top of the cliff a lance with a pennon flying from it, and hard enough he found the climb, unburdened by the weight of a damsel. He said as much when he returned to the castle, and soon, like their lord, all the Count's followers were sure that Edmond could not perform the task he had been set.

The next morning Edmond and Calixte heard mass, and then they walked together to the foot of the cliff, where the Count and all from the castle awaited them. Calixte had eaten nothing since before the hunt the previous day, and she wore her thinnest gown and none of her jewels, hoping that thus she might be as light a burden to Edmond as possible.

The Count looked at Edmond. 'Are you ready? Come, let us see you climb.'

Edmond knelt and kissed Calixte's hand, and then he took her up upon his back and began to climb the cliff. The chalk was loose in places and rolled away beneath his feet, and in others it was slippery. But each time he found a foothold without faltering and he kept his balance, and he climbed upwards without a pause.

The watchers saw him growing smaller and smaller the higher he went. At first they had only surprise that he had climbed so far and so fast; but when he was more than half-way up the six-hundred-foot cliff, their surprise turned to admiration and they began to hope he would perform the feat. What had at first seemed a rather cruel jest of their lord, though they had been ready enough to laugh with him, now became earnest, and to each one of them it was suddenly of great importance that Edmond should not fail. By the time that he was two-thirds of the way up the cliff, all were hoping and even praying that he would succeed, and of all the watchers only the Count was unmoved and scornful still. 'So brave an effort deserves its reward,' said his followers; but they did no more than whisper it, for fear of his wrath.

Higher and higher Edmond climbed without a pause. His back ached and his feet could hardly keep from stumbling, his head was dizzy and his eyes were dim, while the weight he carried seemed almost unbearable. Calixte, all but distraught with

anxiety, spoke encouragingly to him, reminding him of her love for him and telling him many times that there was such a very little way more to go to reach the lance with its pennon flying in the breeze. Yet it seemed to her in reality still so far away. But Edmond had no breath to spare to answer her, and indeed, after a time, he did not even hear her for the clamour of the beating of his heart.

And then, though he did not realize it, there were only a few more yards to go: just a little above him fluttered the pennon. And then at last it was before him and within his grasp, and his dazed eyes saw it there. He stumbled to it, plucked out the lance from the ground and raised it high above his head that all might see he had reached his goal. A great cheer rose from the watchers, caps were thrown into the air, hoods were pulled off and waved in triumph; no one any longer cared if the Count were angered or no. But amidst it all the Count remained unmoved, his eyes still hard and his smile still scornful. Yet he was thinking to himself, 'He is brave, that lad, and strong. My Calixte might have done worse for a husband.'

On the top of the cliff, Calixte, speechless with joy, could find no words to praise her Edmond as he set her down upon the ground. But when she would have put her arms about him and kissed him, there, in sight of all, she saw how the lance fell from his grasp and how he swayed and dropped to his knees. 'Calixte,' he whispered, 'Calixte, my dearest.' And the next moment he lay dead at her feet.

She knelt beside him, calling his name over and over again, as though the sound of her voice might have revived him. But when at last she realized that he could not hear her, she gave a great cry, and then looked wildly about her, as if she feared that there might be someone there to take him from her. She rose, and half dragging, half carrying Edmond, she went to the edge of the cliff; then heaving him upright and clasping him in her arms, she flung both herself and her lover down the slope, while the crowd, with horror, could do no more than watch.

A few moments later the two broken bodies lay at the foot of the cliff, and the Count, no longer unmoved or smiling, covered his face with his hands and prayed God's forgiveness for his pride.

The next day a company of noble knights came to where Edmond's body had been laid in the chapel of the castle. They brought with them the trappings of knighthood: the silken surcoat and the crimson mantle, the hauberk and the helmet. They clad Edmond in them, putting the helmet on his head and fastening the gilded spurs to his feet, and they laid sword and shield beside him. Then the Count, his face drawn and tired, as though he had become an old man in one day, knighted Edmond, even as he had promised. Then Calixte was decked as for a bridal, and she and Edmond were buried side by side.

As for the Count, he gave his wealth to found a monastery and a nunnery, and he went himself on a crusade to the Holy Land; and it is said that he never came home again.

The Hobgoblin and the Washer-girl

and

The Peasant and the Wolf

Here are two folk tales from Savoy, in the Western Alps, both on the subject of curiosity.
First,

The Tale of the Hobgoblin and the Washer-girl

Near the town of Annecy there once stood a large farm-house. On this farm there lived and worked an orphaned servant girl. She was the youngest of all the servants at the farm, and so not only her master and her mistress and their family, but also all the other servants, ordered her about and sent her running here and there all day long. Besides the washing she had many other tasks to do, but none she found so hard or hated so much as the washing. Every week she had to go to the stream which lay some distance from the farm, trudging across the fields with a big basket of dirty linen; and kneeling at the edge of the stream for hour after hour she would rub the never-ending sheets and clothes against the flat stones until they were clean. Then she would rinse them in the water and wring them out and fold them into the basket, before carrying them back to the farm again to spread on the grass to dry.

One day the work seemed even harder than usual, or perhaps it was that she was more tired, but anyhow, the unhappy girl began to weep, her tears dripping on the wet stones and trickling into the stream. 'Oh, why,' she thought, 'oh, why is there no one to help me?'

Suddenly she heard a little squeaking voice close by her. 'What is the matter? Why do you cry?'

She looked all about her, but could see no one, and she was afraid. Yet the voice seemed kindly enough, so she dried her tears, sniffed a little, and answered, 'Because I have always so much work to do and no one to help me.'

'You are a good girl,' said the voice, 'and as you have never harmed or displeased the hobgoblins, I will help you with the washing.'

Her eyes grew very round. 'Are you a hobgoblin?' she asked.

'Indeed I am. What did you suppose?' replied the voice.

'But I cannot see you,' protested the girl.

'Even if you cannot see me, I am here. Watch me.' And at once the girl saw how a sheet was taken from the basket, dipped into the water and laid upon the wet stones; and then, open-mouthed, she saw how it was rubbed and

139

pounded and rinsed and wrung, shaken out and folded neatly, all in a moment or two, by invisible hands.

'Now for another,' said the voice cheerfully, as it took up the next sheet; and when that was clean, the farmer's wife's best chemise was lifted out of the basket. 'She must be large, the one who wears this,' chuckled the voice.

The girl began to laugh, and was no longer afraid; and soon she and her invisible helper were scrubbing and rubbing side by side, and chattering like magpies about everything under the sun. In what seemed like no time at all, the washing was done. 'Off you go now, and put it out to dry,' said the hobgoblin. 'I shall be waiting here for you next week.'

And sure enough, the next week he was waiting for her, and again the week after, and each week after that, until the girl began to look forward to washing days. Each week she thanked the hobgoblin gratefully for his help; but one day she said, 'I wish you were not invisible, I should so much like to see you and know what you look like.'

'That,' said the little voice firmly, 'you may not do.' And though she pleaded with him for many minutes, he would only say no.

But having once become curious to know what her unseen friend looked like, she could have no peace. At night she lay awake in her attic wondering and teasing herself over the matter, and each time she went to the stream with the washing she would beg the hobgoblin to show himself to her. To all his refusals she paid no heed, and soon it became her first greeting to him on washing days, 'Let me see you some time. Please let me.' And at last it came to the point when each time they worked together at the stream, she could talk of nothing else. And so, worn out by her demands, the hobgoblin sighed and said, 'Very well, you shall see me, if you insist. At midnight on Friday come alone to the byre and I shall be there. But make sure you come alone, and tell no one of it. And above all, whatever you see or hear in the byre, take care you do not cross yourself.' And eagerly the girl promised to obey.

On the Friday night she waited impatiently until she heard midnight strike, then she rose from her bed, dressed herself, and tiptoed down to the byre. In the byre it was still and silent except for the breathing of the cows, which were darker shadows in the darkness, and the scurry of the mice rustling in the straw. She looked about her, but she saw nothing strange. Then suddenly she spied, in a corner, her master's big black pig. She had no sooner begun to wonder what the pig should be doing there, when she was aware of how strange it appeared. Its eyes were burning like live coals, its tail seemed more twisted than ever she remembered it, its ears were sharp and alert, while its black body seemed to glow and shine. She was so startled by the sight, that without thinking, she made the sign of the cross, murmuring to herself, 'Heaven help us, what is wrong with the old pig?'

Immediately, the pig gave a terrible cry and vanished. Terrified, the girl ran back to the house and up to her attic, and jumping into bed with her clothes on, hid her head under the blanket.

In the morning the farmer wondered where his black pig

had gone to; but though he searched all day and asked all his neighbours, he never found it, so he swore it must have been taken by thieves in the night. And the washer-girl never told him any differently.

But never again did the hobgoblin come to the stream to help her with the washing, not however hard she cried over her work, and bitterly did she repent of her foolish curiosity.

This, now, is the story of

The Peasant and the Wolf

A long time ago the plain of Bessans was covered by a wide forest. Little is left of that forest today, and this, according to the country folk who dwell there, is the reason.

A poor peasant was one day coming home through the forest, bringing with him the two loaves that he had bought, round rings of black bread which he carried slung one over each arm. He was striding along, whistling merrily to himself, when all of a sudden a huge grey wolf stepped out on to the path before him. The wolf was lean and gaunt, with ribs that showed through its skin, and it opened its mouth to growl at the peasant, showing him the widest throat and the largest teeth that he had ever seen. The unfortunate man stopped dead, overcome with terror. It was useless for him to flee, for he knew that so large a wolf would catch him easily if he tried to run away. For what seemed to him a lifetime, he stood there, staring stupidly, while the wolf came slowly nearer.

Then, in a moment, the man had an idea. 'God bless you, wolf,' he said with chattering teeth. 'You seem hungry. Try some of this good bread.' He broke a piece off one of the loaves and threw it to the wolf, who immediately took up the bread and ate it with obvious enjoyment. While the beast was eating, the peasant slipped by and hurried on his way, congratulating himself on his quick wits.

But he had not gone far when he heard a sound, and he looked round to see the wolf loping after him. 'Heaven help me,' he thought. He broke off another piece of bread and threw it on the path behind him. 'Here is more for you to eat, good wolf.' Then he took to his heels and ran as fast as he could. But his fastest was not fast enough, and soon, once again, he heard the wolf coming after him, and looking back over his shoulder in terror, he saw how it was rapidly catching him up. He stopped and broke off another piece from the loaf and threw it on the path, then once more he ran on. And so it went all through the forest, with the peasant running along in front and the wolf running after him and only failing to catch him because it stopped to eat the bread which he threw down for it.

At last the peasant, quite exhausted, reached the edge of the forest and saw his cottage with his wife standing at the door, watching for him, and he gave a great sigh of relief, for his legs were fast failing him, and he had, besides, no more than one piece of bread left. He stumbled up to the cottage door and leant panting against the door-post. 'Why, husband, whatever is the matter?' asked his wife. 'Did you meet with a witch or a hobgoblin in the forest? And where is the bread you went to buy?'

He had no breath left to answer her, and only gestured towards the trees, where the wolf was now appearing, bounding in the direction of the cottage, its red tongue hanging out, considerably plumper than when the peasant had first met it.

'A wolf!' she cried. 'The wicked creature! Small wonder you ran like a madman. What a mercy it did not catch you.'

'I gave it the bread to eat,' gasped the peasant, unable, exhausted though he was, to forbear from grinning at the remembrance of his cunning.

'Good bread wasted on a wicked wolf!' exclaimed his wife. 'I never heard such a thing in my life.' Now, she was really very fond of her husband, and she was very glad to see him come safely home after his adventure, but she was also very hungry, and had been looking forward all day to a slice or two of fresh black bread to eat with her broth of carrots and cabbage. She looked at the wolf. 'You had best come indoors,' she snapped, 'or that brute will finish its supper with a mouthful of you.' She stamped into the cottage and the peasant went after her, but before he closed the door he looked at the piece of bread in his hands, all that was left of two large loaves. He grinned and shrugged his shoulders. 'You may as well finish it,' he said. 'God keep you, wolf.' And he threw the last of the bread to the beast and closed and bolted the door.

The wolf ate the bread and waited a while outside the cottage, and all the time the voice of the peasant's wife could be heard through the shut door, railing at her husband and wishing an ill fate on the wolf, as they sat down to eat their broth without any bread. When at last she ceased and all was quiet again in the cottage, the wolf returned to the forest like a grey shadow.

Many months later, by means of much hard work, the peasant and his wife had managed to save enough to buy themselves a cow, and one morning the man set off through the forest to the fair at Bourg Saint Maurice, where he hoped to find an old cow going cheaply, for he had not enough money to buy anything better. In the town he walked about looking at the cattle offered for sale, hoping to make a bargain. All of a sudden a tall, thin stranger, well dressed in grey, with a long face and a pointed chin and close-set eyes, stood before him. 'You wish to buy a cow?' he asked.

'I do, indeed, sir,' replied the peasant. 'But it is a problem, since I have little to spend.'

'In my byre,' said the stranger, 'I have many cows. Perhaps one of them would be to your liking.'

They went together to a fine house, and in the byre behind it there were, as the stranger had said, many cows. 'Choose the very best of all,' invited the stranger, 'and I will give her to you as a gift.'

The peasant was astonished, but since such luck does not come one's way every day, he quickly chose that cow which seemed to him to be the best. The stranger smiled, showing large white teeth. 'You have chosen wisely.' He tied a rope about the cow's neck and handed the rope to the peasant. 'She is yours,' he said, 'and may she give you plentiful milk for many years.' He put his hand into his pocket and pulled out a little box. 'This,' he said, 'is a gift for your wife. Be sure that she opens it herself, and when she is alone.' The peasant, wondering, took the box, and the stranger led him to the street.

'But why,' asked the bewildered peasant, 'are you doing this kindness to me?'

The stranger smiled again. 'Do you remember how you once showed kindness to a wolf in the forest and fed him with two loaves? Well, I was that wolf, and I always return kindness with kindness and cruelty with cruelty. Now good-bye, my friend, God be with you.'

Amazed and delighted, the peasant set off through the forest for home, leading his cow and carrying the little box. Soon he began to wonder what could be in the box, and with every step he took his curiosity grew greater, until at last he stopped altogether, turning the box this way and that, shaking it and sniffing at it, to see if he could guess what it held. 'He said that she must open it herself, and when she is alone,' he thought, 'and she will surely tell me what is in it when she has found out for herself, and then I also shall know. Indeed, it is her duty to tell me what is in the box, for a good wife should have no secrets from her husband, and that being so, there could be no harm in my having a peep inside first.'

He sat down beneath a young larch-tree while the cow grazed a little way off, and carefully he opened the box. He dropped it instantly and sprang to his feet in a great fright, for out of the box leapt a tall flame which set fire to a branch of the larch-tree. 'Had it been my wife who opened it,' thought the peasant, 'her hair and her cap would have caught fire and she would perhaps have been burnt to death.'

He saw how the larch-tree was burning fiercely, and having no idea how to put out a fire in a tree, he hurried off home with his cow, very thankful that he had given way to his curiosity and opened the box.

From the larch-tree the fire spread to the whole forest of Bessans, and the greater part of it was burnt to ashes; but the peasant and his wife lived on happily in their cottage with the cow, which was by far the best in the whole district.

After those two stories, one may wonder whether it is more profitable, in Savoy, to be inquisitive or not.

The Prince of the Seven Golden Cows

A LONG time ago there lived in a town in Gascony a
prince who had for his coat of arms seven golden
cows, and from this he was known as the Prince of
the Seven Golden Cows. He was very rich, and of all men
in Gascony he was the most generous. Every morning of
his life he went to hear mass, and on leaving the church he
would find all the beggars and the poor of the town awaiting him on the church steps, and to each one of them he
would give liberally, day after day, so that they would
call to heaven to witness his charity and declare, 'Prince
of the Seven Golden Cows, there is no one like you in all
the world. For your sake we would go through fire and
water.'

Every evening of his life he would feast with his friends:
the noblemen and the well-to-do merchants of the town.
At his tables were good food and good Gascon wine in
abundance, and no guest ever left his castle without a fine

gift to carry home; so that they would call to heaven to witness his splendour and his bounty and declare, 'Prince of the Seven Golden Cows, there is no one like you in all the world. For your sake we would go through fire and water.'

One day a young man came to the castle and asked to speak with the Prince. He said, 'I have heard of your kindness and I am come to beg a favour. There is surely in all this town no one more unfortunate than I. When I was seven years old, my father and my mother died, and since that day I have worked hard to earn my keep. For a few happy months I have been betrothed to a maiden, as good as she was lovely, and we were soon to have married. But this morning she died, and I think that I shall never be happy again. If I knew enough Latin to read the prayers in the prayer book, I would become a monk, but I know no Latin. Have pity on me, Prince of the Seven Golden Cows, and give me fifteen crowns to buy mourning.'

'My friend,' said the Prince of the Seven Golden Cows, 'I am indeed sorry for you. You shall have not fifteen, but one hundred crowns, and may you meet with no more misfortunes.'

The young man thanked the Prince of the Seven Golden Cows and went, taking with him the hundred crowns. But after three days he returned, wearing mourning. 'Prince of the Seven Golden Cows,' he said, 'you have been kind to me. There is nothing else for me to live for. Let me be your servant and dwell in your castle, and I will serve you faithfully and ask no wage.'

'I would not ask any man's service without paying him

his hire,' said the Prince. 'But if that is as you wish it, it shall be so.'

In that manner the young man became a servant in the castle of the Prince of the Seven Golden Cows, and so well he worked and so loyal he showed himself, that the Prince set him over all his other servants. But always the young man wore mourning, so that he came to be known as the Black Steward.

One day he came to the Prince of the Seven Golden Cows. 'Lord,' he said, 'you spend too much on your guests, and you give too much in charity. Within a year your coffers will be empty of gold and silver, and you will be ruined.'

'What does that matter?' asked the Prince of the Seven Golden Cows. 'I have neither wife nor child to be my heir. I shall spend my gold until it is gone. And when that day comes, I shall still be rich enough, for I have many good friends who will not see me want. Time after time have they told me that for my sake they would go through fire and water.'

'You cannot be certain of that,' said the Black Steward.

That evening, as they feasted, the Prince of the Seven Golden Cows said to his guests, 'Often have you all said to me that you would go through fire and water for my sake, yet today the Black Steward has told me that I cannot be sure of it. How do you answer him, my friends?'

And they one and all cried out against the Black Steward, calling him a rogue. 'He steals from you and he cheats you and he cannot be trusted,' they said.

The Prince of the Seven Golden Cows sent for the Black

Steward. 'My friends have called you a thief who steals from his master. Tell me, Black Steward, are they speaking the truth?'

The Black Steward denied nothing. 'It is true. I have stolen from you, lord.'

In anger the Prince of the Seven Golden Cows drove the Black Steward from his castle, bidding him begone for ever. And the Black Steward, who had indeed robbed his master of enough gold to buy a castle, went far from the town to where the River Gers flowed slowly and sleepily past the meadows and vineyards of Gascony; and there, on the bank of the river, he bought a castle and the land around it, and in the castle he waited for what he knew would come to pass.

When a year was all but gone, the Prince of the Seven Golden Cows saw that his coffers were empty and knew that he was ruined. He gave a last banquet for his guests; and when the feasting was over, he said, 'My friends, my coffers are all empty and my gold and my silver are spent, and I have nothing left to offer you. So many times have you said to me that for my sake you would go through fire and water. Now that I am ruined, give me your help.'

But his guests looked at one another, and their looks were dark and they scowled. 'Prince of the Seven Golden Cows,' they said, 'you have wasted your wealth in alms-giving. Go, ask the poor for help, not us.'

The Prince of the Seven Golden Cows could hardly believe he had heard aright; but when he saw how they turned their backs on him and spoke amongst themselves as though he were not there, he knew that he was not mistaken. He went out to the poor and the beggars, and they called to him for alms. 'My friends,' he said, 'I can give you nothing, for I have nothing left to give. My coffers are all empty and my gold and my silver are spent. But so many times have you told me that for my sake you would go through fire and water that I have no fears for the future. You are poor, my friends, and you have little, yet will you not share that little with me?'

But the beggars all cried out against him, saying, 'You have squandered your wealth in food and wine and in feasting with your guests. Why should we share with you the little we have? Go, beg your bread, even as we do.'

The Prince of the Seven Golden Cows could hardly believe he had heard aright; but when he saw how the beggars muttered together, cursing him and shaking their fists because he had nothing to give them, he knew that he was not mistaken.

He stood sadly in his courtyard, crushed between the scorn of his guests and the blame of the poor; and then there came a great clattering of hoofs from the street outside and the baying of many hounds, and into the courtyard rode the Black Steward, a big cudgel in his hands and a pack of huge hounds at his horse's heels.

'After them! Away with them!' cried the Black Steward to the hounds; and they ran, biting and snarling, among the beggars and the noblemen and the well-to-do merchants, whilst the Black Steward himself laid about him with his cudgel, until the courtyard was clear. Then he dismounted and went to where his master stood. 'Lord,' he said, 'they were ungrateful, so I have driven them away.'

But the Prince of the Seven Golden Cows looked coldly at the Black Steward. 'I ask no services from one who has robbed me,' he said.

'Lord, I robbed you that there might be something left to you when you were ruined. On the bank of the River Gers there stands a castle which awaits the arrival of its lord. It is yours.'

So the Prince of the Seven Golden Cows left the town for ever and went to live in the castle on the quiet bank of the Gers, and there the Black Steward served him without wages, even as he had done in the old days. And so things went on for seven years.

Then, on the last evening of the seventh year, the Prince of the Seven Golden Cows sent for the Black Steward. 'In all my life,' he said, 'I have found but one loyal friend, and that is you. I would tell you my great secret, that you may profit from it when I am gone. Seven years ago, when my coffers were empty and I had spent all my gold and silver on the giving of alms to those who were thankless and on the feasting of those I believed my friends, I could, had I wished, have gained more riches to replace all I had lost. Yet this I did not do, because I had at last learnt the ingratitude of all men save yourself. But now I am growing old, and within a year I shall be dead. I would wish you, my only friend, to be my heir, so I will tell you the secret of the Seven Golden Cows which are the device of my house. First, fetch an axe, then saddle two horses, and we shall ride forth together.'

The Black Steward fetched an axe and saddled two horses, and he and the Prince of the Seven Golden Cows rode out of the castle into the winter's evening. At midnight they reached a cross-roads, close by a marsh where many reeds grew.

'Take your axe,' said the Prince of the Seven Golden Cows to the Black Steward, 'and cut the tallest of the reeds. But take care, for the reed will seek to protect itself, and it will change its shape three times whilst you are cutting it. Three times only may you strike with your axe, and if by the third stroke you have not cut the reed, you will die in that instant.'

The Black Steward took his axe, and going to the tallest of the reeds, he grasped it firmly and raised the axe. At once the reed changed into a serpent with seven hissing heads. But the Black Steward struck boldly, for all the fearsome sight. When he raised his axe for the second stroke, he saw how the reed had become a new-born child. For a moment only he hesitated, then he struck boldly. As he raised his axe for the third stroke, the reed took the likeness of his long-dead betrothed, and the Black Steward trembled and the axe almost dropped from his hand. But he remembered the warning of the Prince of the Seven Golden Cows, and he summoned up all his strength and his courage, and he struck boldly for the last time. And in his left hand he held the tallest of the reeds, severed at the root. He returned to his master.

'You have done well,' said the Prince of the Seven Golden Cows. 'Now cut from the reed enough to make a flute.' When this was done, they returned to the castle.

For the next five months, every night, when the servants of the castle slept, the Prince of the Seven Golden Cows taught the Black Steward a certain tune to play on the flute. And when mid-June was come, and the eve of St John, the Prince said, 'At midnight, bring two cauldrons, six leathern sacks, and the flute, and come with me to the meadow by the river.'

At midnight, with the flute, the cauldrons, and the sacks, they stood on the bank of the Gers. 'Now play on the flute the tune which I taught you,' said the Prince of the Seven Golden Cows.

The Black Steward did as he was bidden, and at once the ground opened, and out of the earth came seven golden cows. They bowed their heads before the Prince and waited. 'Milk the cows into the cauldrons,' he ordered. So the Black Steward milked the cows into the cauldrons until the cauldrons were full; and the milk of the seven golden cows was golden coins.

'Now fill the sacks with the gold,' said the Prince. When it was done, the Prince of the Seven Golden Cows showed the Black Steward a certain spot in the river. 'Throw the sacks into the water,' he said. As the last sack sank under the water, it was dawn, and the earth opened and the golden cows disappeared.

A month later, the Prince of the Seven Golden Cows was dead, even as he had said. The Black Steward saw him buried with all the splendour fitting to his rank, and then he went to the castle in the town where the Prince had spent his wealth in feasting his guests and in giving alms, and from there he had the news cried about the streets that the Prince of the Seven Golden Cows was dead, and that he had died rich.

At once the noblemen and the well-to-do merchants and the beggars flocked to the castle. 'How sad the news! The good Prince of the Seven Golden Cows, there was no one like him in all the world. For his sake we would have gone through fire and water. Perhaps he has remembered us in his will,' they said as they crowded in the courtyard.

Then the door of the castle opened and the Black Steward rode forth, his big cudgel in his hands and his hounds at his horse's heels. 'After them! Away with them!' he cried to the hounds. And the hounds ran, biting and snarling, among the noblemen and the merchants and the beggars, whilst the Black Steward laid about him with his cudgel until the courtyard was empty. 'Let that be the legacy of the Prince of the Seven Golden Cows,' he said.

Then the Black Steward returned to the place where the Prince of the Seven Golden Cows was buried, and he studied and learnt Latin. And when he knew enough Latin to read the prayers in the prayer book, he became a monk; and with the gold from the River Gers he built a monastery, where night and day he prayed for the soul of his master, the Prince of the Seven Golden Cows.

FRENCH FAIRY STORIES

The Ship that Sailed on Land

THERE was once a king who ruled over a large kingdom. He had all the pleasant things which money
can buy, and he had, moreover, a daughter who was
the most beautiful maiden in all his land. But in spite of
his power and his riches, and in spite of his affection for his
daughter, he was surly and discontented, and he grumbled
night and day because amongst all his treasures he had not
a ship which could sail on the land as well as over the
water.

At last he issued a proclamation that he would give the
hand of his daughter and half his riches to the man who
could bring him such a ship. His messengers went all about
his kingdom reading the proclamation in every market
square and on every village green, but no one of all those
who heard it had any idea where such a ship was to be
found.

Now, on the edge of a forest there lived three brothers,

159

the sons of a wood-cutter, who earned a bare living by cutting wood for other people's fires. When they heard the proclamation they all three said, 'It would be a fine thing to marry the Princess and have half the riches of the King.' And the eldest brother took up his axe, a loaf, a goats' milk cheese, and a jug of wine. 'I am going to try my hand at making this ship,' he said, and went off alone into the forest.

In the forest he chose out a tall oak-tree and set to work to fell it, and so hard did he work that before long it lay on the ground before him. Well pleased with the result of his labours, he sat down to rest himself and eat his bread and cheese and drink his wine in the shade. While he ate, a magpie flew on to a tree near by, and there it hopped from branch to branch, chattering and clacking, 'Save a little for me! Save a little for me!'

The eldest brother looked up. 'Go away, you noisy creature. I have no food to waste on you.' And he went on eating.

The magpie came nearer. 'What will you be making, wood-cutter, out of that fine tree?'

'What is that to you?' replied the eldest brother, annoyed. He laughed mockingly. 'If you must have an answer, I shall be making spoons.'

'Spoons!' said the magpie. 'Spoons! Spoons!' And it flew away clacking, 'Spoons! Spoons! Spoons!'

When he had rested, the eldest brother took up his axe and set to work again, but each piece of wood he cut from the tree he had felled became at once a spoon. He hacked away with all his might, but the harder he worked, the

160

faster came the spoons, until he was standing in a heap of wooden spoons right up to his knees. Large ladles to stir a pot of soup, little spoons for salt, spoons for cooking, spoons for eating with, everywhere were spoons; until at last he flung down his axe in despair and went home.

'How did you fare?' asked his brothers.

'I think, after all, that I would not care to marry the Princess,' said the eldest brother, and he would say no more.

'It would please me well enough,' said the second brother. And the next day he took his axe and a loaf and a goats' milk cheese and a jug of wine and went into the forest. It happened to him as to his brother, and when he had chosen and felled his tree and was sitting down to eat his bread and cheese and drink his wine, the magpie came with a great chattering, 'Save a little for me! Save a little for me!'

'Away with you, you feathered thief. I have no food to spare for you.'

'What will you be making, wood-cutter, out of that fine tree?'

'What is that to you?' replied the second brother, annoyed. He sneered. 'If you must have an answer, I shall be making spindles.'

'Spindles! Spindles!' said the magpie. And it flew away clacking, 'Spindles! Spindles!'

When the second brother set to work again, every piece of wood he cut turned into a spindle, until he stood knee deep in spindles, large, small, and middling sized; and then, in despair, he flung down his axe and went home. 'I think, after all,' he said to his brothers, 'I would not care to marry the Princess.' But more he would not say.

The next day the youngest brother took his axe and a loaf and a goat's milk cheese and a jug of wine and went out to the forest. And it happened to him as to his brothers, and when he had chosen and felled his tree, and was sitting eating his bread and cheese and drinking his wine, the magpie came chattering, 'Save a little for me! Save a little for me!'

The youngest brother looked up and smiled. 'You are welcome to share with me,' he said. And he scattered crumbs and bits of cheese on the ground for the magpie, who quickly pecked them up. 'What will you be making, wood-cutter, out of that fine tree?'

'I should like, if I have skill enough, to make a ship which will sail on the land as well as over the water, so that I may take it to the King and win his daughter and half his riches.'

'A ship which will sail on the land! A ship which will sail on the land!' said the magpie. And it flew away clacking, 'A ship which will sail on the land! A ship which will sail on the land!'

When the youngest brother set to work again, every piece of wood he cut became part of a ship: keel, ribs, stem, and stern, as they fell to the ground they sprang into place of themselves; so that in a very short while the tree had become a ship, complete with mast and sail, decorated with carving all about her sides and with a figure-head at her prow.

The young wood-cutter jumped into the ship, gave a

word of command, and away the ship went, sailing merrily over meadow and moorland, hill and dale, towards the palace of the King.

On the way the wood-cutter saw a man sitting by the wayside. He had a great mouth as wide as an oven-door, full of huge teeth, and he was gnawing at a dry bone as hungrily as any stray dog. 'Why do you do that, my friend?' asked the wood-cutter.

'I am hungry,' replied the man. 'But I have spent all my money on food, and can buy no more.'

'I am going to the palace of the King,' said the wood-cutter. 'There should be food enough in a king's palace. Come along with me, and perhaps I can help you to something to eat.'

The man threw away his bone and jumped into the ship, and off they went together, the hungry man and the young wood-cutter.

A little way on they came to a stream. A man knelt beside it drinking the water as fast as he could. While they watched him the water grew lower and lower until the stream was dry, and all in a matter of moments. 'Why do you do that, my friend?' asked the wood-cutter.

'I am thirsty,' replied the man, 'and I cannot afford wine, for times have been bad with me.'

'In the palace of the King there should be wine enough. Come with me, and I may be able to help you.'

The man jumped into the ship, and away they went together, the hungry man, the thirsty man, and the young wood-cutter.

A little way farther on, they came upon a strange sight:

a young man with shoulders as broad as you have ever seen, walking along carrying half a forest on his back. 'Why are you doing that, my friend?' the wood-cutter called out.

The young man grinned. 'I am tired of my stepmother's nagging. She always complains that I never bring home enough wood for the fire. So today I thought that I would take her half the forest.'

'That should content her,' said the wood-cutter.

The young man laughed. 'You do not know my stepmother,' he said.

'If you would be quit of your stepmother,' said the wood-cutter, 'come with me. For I am going to the palace of the King, and I doubt if she would think to look for you there.'

The young man threw down the trees he carried, all save one oak, and jumped into the ship. And away they went together, the hungry man, the thirsty man, the strong man, and the young wood-cutter.

A little way along they saw an even stranger sight. A man with a pair of bellows as large as a house was standing in the middle of a hayfield blowing away hard with his bellows up into the sky. 'Why are you doing that, my friend?' asked the wood-cutter.

'I am blowing away the rain clouds, so that my master's hay harvest may not be spoilt. And a tedious task it is to be sure, and small thanks does he give me for it.'

'Then come with me to the palace of the King, and maybe I can find other work for you,' said the wood-cutter.

The man jumped into the ship with his bellows, and

away they went together, the hungry man, the thirsty man, the strong man, the man with the bellows, and the young wood-cutter.

At last they came to the palace, and there the wood-cutter offered the ship to the King; and when the King saw that the ship could indeed sail upon the land as well as over the water, he was, you may be sure, very pleased. But he looked at the wood-cutter and thought to himself, 'A wood-cutter is hardly a fitting bridegroom for my only daughter,' and he searched in his mind for some way of evading his promise.

'No doubt you are thinking that now you have brought me the ship you have won the Princess for your wife,' he said to the wood-cutter. 'And so you have. But there is still a little matter to be settled. In my larders are ten roasted oxen, ready for eating. We want no cold meats for the wedding-feast, but until they are cleared from the spits, we can roast no more. If you and your men can eat them, all ten, by tonight, then we can talk of the marriage.'

'That is easily done, your majesty.' And the wood-cutter nodded to the hungry man, who had been waiting for just such a chance, and he was away to the kitchen in a moment, and back again, long before sundown, licking his lips. 'That was the first good meal I have had in my life,' he said. 'Many thanks, your majesty.'

The King frowned. 'After eating comes drinking,' he said to the wood-cutter. 'In my cellar are ten barrels of wine. It is a little sour, and therefore unfitted for a wedding, but until the barrels are emptied, new wine cannot be poured in.'

'They will be easily emptied, your majesty,' interrupted the young wood-cutter, and he nodded to the thirsty man, who had been listening to the King's words eagerly. Away he ran to the cellar, and was with them again in an hour or two, wiping his mouth with the back of his hand. 'At last

my thirst is almost quenched—for the time being, at any rate. And I remembered to drink your majesty's health.'

But by now the King was really angry, and he called out his soldiers. First the foot soldiers came running, swords in hand, a truly fearsome sight. But the strong man stepped forward. 'Just leave them to me,' he said to the wood-cutter. And holding his oak-tree by the trunk, he swept the soldiers away with the leafy branches as easily as a housewife sweeps dust off a floor with a broom.

Then the cavalry came charging, horses neighing and swords flashing, enough to terrify the bravest heart. 'This is my task,' said the man with the bellows to the young wood-cutter. And he puffed with his bellows and away the cavalry was blown, men, horses, swords, and all.

'Stop, stop!' called the King. 'I give you my daughter, and you shall marry her tomorrow.'

So the young wood-cutter married the Princess and had half the King's riches beside; and he did not forget his four companions. And you may be sure that the hungry man was never hungry again, nor the thirsty man thirsty; while the strong man never needed to go home to live with his stepmother, and the man with the bellows found better ways of spending his time than by blowing away the rain clouds from any master's fields.

Ripopet-Barabas

A PRETTY peasant girl once lived with her mother and her brothers close by the palace of a king. One summer's day, at hay-harvest time, her mother gave her a plate of pancakes to take to her brothers who were working in the fields. The girl put the plate into a basket and set off, clop, clop in her wooden sabots. As she went on her way she opened the basket, and having nothing better to do to pass the time as she walked along, she took out a pancake and, folding it twice, nibbled it all around the edge and at the centre, and bit it through in every other part with her little white teeth. Then she unfolded it to see the pattern she had made and was delighted with the result. She held it up to look at the sun through the holes, she turned it this way and that to admire it, standing stock still in the roadway and quite forgetting her brothers' mid-day meal.

At that moment the son of the King came riding by,

and he reined in his horse and spoke to her. 'That is exquisite lace you have there. Did you make it yourself?'

The girl blushed and could think of nothing to answer him, so she stood there, looking at the ground and holding the bitten pancake behind her back, while with her other hand she clutched tightly to her basket.

The Prince was charmed by what he believed to be her modesty over her skill, and he was, moreover, charmed to see how pretty she was, and he said, 'My mother the Queen has many lace-makers, but none of them works so well as you. If you will come with me to the palace she will be pleased to have you work for her.'

The girl looked up, meaning to refuse with no delay, but in the moment she glimpsed the kindly, smiling face of the young Prince, she knew that she could not bear to see him perhaps never again. So instead she dropped him a curtsy and said, 'You do me much honour, your highness.' And she went to the palace with him.

But once at the palace, with pillow and bobbins set before her, she became afraid. She longed to explain that it had been all a mistake and that she had no idea of how to make lace, yet she dared not, for fear of the Queen's anger; and besides, by this time, she knew that she loved the Prince and would never love anyone else.

In the little room she had been given, with the lace-making pillow fallen to the floor, and bobbins and pins and the white linen thread lying idle beside her, she sat and wept and wept. All of a sudden she heard a noise in the chimney, and looking up, saw a goblin jump down into the hearth. Terrified, she sprang to her feet and would have run from the room, but he called to her, 'Never fear me, pretty one. I am Ripopet-Barabas, and I mean you no harm. If you will promise to be my wife, a year from to-day, I will give you the skill which you lack, and no one in the whole land shall make finer lace than yours.'

While she hesitated, twisting her hands in her apron, he laughed. 'Come,' he said, 'take my gift, and I will make a bargain with you. For a year you shall be the best lace-maker in the land, and then I shall come to you once again, and if you have not forgotten my name I shall demand no other payment from you. But if you have forgotten it, then you must come with me and be my wife.'

Now, the poor girl had been so frightened that she had not even heard his name, let alone forgotten it; but she thought of the handsome young Prince, and she thought how, in a year, she must surely remember the goblin's name, so she said, 'Let it be as you say.'

And the goblin laughed again and sprang up the chimney and vanished from sight.

From that moment the girl found that she could make lace more fine and lovely than could anyone else in the land, and the Queen had no words with which to praise her skill. All day long she would make lace for the Queen, and often while she worked the Prince would come and sit by her and talk to her, and the more he saw of her, the more he liked her company.

And so the first eleven months of the year passed very pleasantly, and then, when there were no more than thirty days left before the goblin would come again, the girl was overcome by fear. She grew pale and thin, so that the

Prince and the Queen became troubled on her account; and
at last, as the month drew to its close, she took to her bed
and lay there, at one moment trembling and at another
weeping as though she could never cease, so that the Queen
thought that she was surely dying, and sent for the court
physician and all the doctors who lived in the land. But
none of them could name her malady. At last an old
woman who was wise and could see farther than most
others, came to the palace to offer her help, and after she
had looked at the girl she said, 'At the end of the palace
gardens is a spring. If she
drinks a cup of water from
that spring, she will recover.'

Immediately, the Queen
sent out a serving-woman
to fetch a cup of water from
the spring; but when the
woman came close to the
spring, she saw a group of
goblins who danced around
a tree near by, singing at
the tops of their little voices.
Astonished and amused by
the strange sight, she forgot
her errand, and stood watching them, unnoticed.

When the serving-
woman did not return with
the water, the Queen herself
hurried out of the palace to

see what was amiss; and when she saw the goblins and heard them singing, she, too, forgot the water which was to cure the girl, and stood watching them, for she had never seen such a sight in her life.

The Prince remained by the bedside of the peasant girl whom he had grown to love, impatiently waiting until someone should bring the cup of water, but when neither the Queen nor the servant returned, he could wait no longer. 'I shall go myself and fetch water from the spring for you,' he said. 'And then you will be cured.'

She smiled at him faintly but with hope, and lay back upon the pillows, waiting. But the minutes passed and the minutes passed, and, like the others, he did not return. And at last the poor girl thought, 'How a cup of water from a spring can help me remember the goblin's name, I do not know. Yet I will not go without a struggle to be a goblin's wife, and I will not lose my prince without a fight.' And she rose up from her bed, and wrapping a cloak around herself, with knees which were almost too weak to support her, walked very slowly and feebly out of the palace and into the garden.

When she came to the spring at the end of the garden, there she saw the Prince and the Queen and the serving-woman, all standing watching the goblins and listening to their singing. Astonished, she watched them also; and then she heard the words of their song.

> We'll brew and bake,
> And make a cake,
> For the bride who comes tomorrow.
>
> We'll sing and dance,
> And leap and prance,
> At the wedding of Ripopet-Barabas.

Immediately she heard the name, the girl gave a little cry of joy, and instantly she was well again, to the great happiness of the King and the Queen and everyone in the palace; but of course, most of all to the great happiness of the Prince.

The year being up on the very next day, the goblin came to fetch his bride, sliding down the chimney of her room. But this time she stood up and faced him boldly. 'Away with you, Ripopet-Barabas. It is the young Prince whom I love, and I will not marry you.'

Furious, the goblin disappeared up the chimney with a howl of rage, and she never saw him again.

A little while later, with the approval of both the King and the Queen, the Prince asked the girl to be his wife. And you may be sure that she did not refuse him.

The Singing Sea, the Dancing Apple,
and
the Bird Which Told the Truth

A KING whose queen had died, leaving him with one son, remarried after many years of mourning. The new queen was young and proud, and she loved nothing so much as power, wishing everyone to respect and obey her, even if everyone could not like her; and what she wished, she in time achieved. When his son was some twenty years old, the King died and the Prince succeeded him. The young King and the widow-Queen had no quarrel with each other: she had no children of her own, so she did not resent him, and for his part, his own mother had died when he was too young to remember her, so his stepmother seemed well enough to his mind.

When he had been king for a number of years, as he was hunting one morning, he overheard the three daughters of a farmer talking together as they worked in their father's field. They were talking of the dreams they had had the night before.

'I dreamt,' said the eldest daughter, 'that I married a baker.'

'I,' said the second daughter, 'dreamt that I married a huntsman.'

But the youngest daughter was silent.

'What did you dream last night?' asked her sisters.

'I dreamt that I married the King,' she replied, 'and that I was the mother of twins: a little prince and a little princess, as beautiful as flowers.'

The King rode up to the three daughters and looked long at the youngest. 'And so you shall be,' he said at last.

Perhaps he was dazzled by her beauty, for she was very lovely; or perhaps he was feeling happy that morning and wished to be even happier; or perhaps it was merely that he was becoming a little tired of always hearing his stepmother order the servants about. But whatever the reason, he took the youngest daughter up on his horse and rode away to his castle by the seashore, and without asking the advice of anyone, he married her there and then.

It is easy to imagine how angry the widow-Queen was. No longer would she rule in the King's household, no longer would she receive his guests with pomp and dignity, no longer would she be the first lady in the land; and worst in her eyes, in all these things she had been supplanted by a farmer's daughter and not by a princess or even by a noblewoman. But she hid her anger and welcomed the new Queen kindly, and praised her stepson's choice of a bride; and plotted and planned continually in her mind, while she smiled and spoke fair words.

When the King had been married for a year, he had to go to war, and as he bade farewell to his queen, she said to him, 'By the time you return, I shall be the mother of twins: a little prince and a little princess, as beautiful as flowers.'

He kissed her and said, 'When they are born, send me a messenger to tell me of it.'

A month later twins were born to the young Queen: a little prince and a little princess, as beautiful as flowers. 'Send a message for me to my husband the King, telling him of it,' she asked the widow-Queen.

'It shall be done,' the stepmother promised.

She sent for a messenger and she told him, 'The Queen bids you go to her husband the King and tell him that a lion cub and a young crocodile have been born to her. And bring his reply to me.'

The messenger did as he was bidden and went to the King where he fought with his army, and gave him the message which he believed to have come from the young Queen. The King grew pale. 'It is sorcery,' he thought. 'For how else should I be the father of a lion cub and a young crocodile?' But aloud he said to the messenger, 'Return to the Queen and tell her to do nothing in this matter until I am home.'

The messenger returned to the castle and told the King's words to the widow-Queen, and she gave him a purse of gold and commanded him to go from the kingdom and never return, on pain of death. Then she went to the young

Queen, where she sat with her two babes in her arms, smiling at them. 'Alas, my poor daughter,' she said. 'The King has received your message and has sent his answer back: "The little Prince and the little Princess, as beautiful as flowers, let them be drowned before I return." What will you do, my poor daughter?'

The young Queen wept, and held her babes close as though she would hide them from all harm. And then at last she said, 'He is the King, and he must be obeyed.' And she rose and wrapped the little Prince and the little Princess in silk and cloth of gold, and laid them in a basket. Then after kissing them for the last time, she gave the basket to a servant and bade him take it down to the seashore and throw it into the sea. The servant took the basket down to the seashore and flung it far out into the sea, and without another glance, returned to the castle.

A month later the war was over and the King came home. His stepmother greeted him at the castle doors. 'Where is my wife the Queen, and the lion cub and the young crocodile who are her children?'

'Alas, my poor son,' said the widow-Queen. 'Her children were no lion cub or young crocodile. They were a little prince and a little princess, as beautiful as flowers. But that terrible woman who is your wife, she had them laid in a basket and thrown into the sea.'

Distraught, the King exclaimed, 'She has murdered our children. Let me never see her face again.' And he ordered her to be locked up in a tall tower of the castle, for he had not the heart to put her to death. 'Never speak of her again,' he said.

And the widow-Queen smiled in triumph and took once more her place as mistress of the castle, the first lady in the land.

But the little Prince and the little Princess had not drowned. The basket had floated on the waves, and many miles along the coast, a poor old fisherman had found it while fishing from his boat. He had carried it home with him. 'Wife, one thing only have we lacked to bless our days. Heaven sent us no children. But now in our old age heaven has sent us twins. See, a little boy and a little girl, as beautiful as flowers.'

For seven years the old fisherman and his wife cared for the twins, loving them as though they had been their own.

But the fisherman was very old, and past his work, and he caught fewer fish each time he sailed out in his little boat, and so had fewer fish to sell, and less money to spend each day, so that in time it became hard for him to find enough to feed four mouths.

'Good father, kind mother,' said the little Prince and the little Princess, 'let us go and seek our fortunes that you may have comfort in your old age.'

'You are too young,' said the fisherman and his wife. But the little Prince and the little Princess pleaded, so that at last the old folk consented. But before they set off the fisherman said, 'It is right that you should know that we are not your parents. Seven years ago I found you floating in a basket on the sea, wrapped in fine silks and cloth of gold.'

Early one morning the twins bade the fisherman and his wife farewell and left them. They walked together along the seashore, on and on. Suddenly the little Princess said, 'Listen, brother, I can hear a voice.'

And they stopped and listened and heard how the sea was singing to them. 'Little Prince, little Princess, as beautiful as flowers, go on walking, go on walking until you find the dancing apple and the bird which tells the truth. Go on walking, go on walking, little Prince, little Princess, as beautiful as flowers.'

So the little Prince and the little Princess went on walking, on and on. They walked for three days and three nights, and then they sat down to rest beneath a tree which was growing near the shore. The little Princess, lying beneath the tree, looked up into its branches. 'See, brother, that apple, red as blood, at the very top of the tree.'

179

And because his sister was hungry, the little Prince climbed up into the tree and picked the apple for her. But as she was about to take a bite from it, a bird flew down and perched upon the little Prince's shoulder. 'Little Princess,' said the bird, 'that is the dancing apple. Do not eat it. Some day you will find the wicked one who had you thrown into the sea to drown, and it is the dancing apple that will show her to you, while I shall tell all the truth. Go on walking, go on walking until you come to a castle, and there you may ask for alms.'

So the little Prince and the little Princess walked on and on, taking with them the dancing apple and the bird which told the truth, until they came to the castle of the King, close by the seashore. And there at the door of the castle they begged for alms. 'There are two children begging at the door,' said the servants to the King.

'Give them all the food they wish for,' ordered the King.

When it had been done, and when they had eaten, the little Prince and the little Princess asked if they might thank the King, and they were brought to him, where he sat with his stepmother at his side. He looked at them with pity. 'You are young to be wandering about the world alone, little ones.'

'Your majesty, we are seeking our fortunes, that our foster parents may have some comfort in their old age. Seven years ago they took us from the sea where we were floating in a basket, wrapped in fine silks and cloth of gold, and have cared kindly for us ever since. We have here with us the bird which tells the truth and the dancing apple. When we find the one who had us thrown into the sea to drown, the apple will show her to us and the bird will tell the truth.'

'Seven years ago,' said the King, much moved, 'my children, a little prince and a little princess, as beautiful as flowers, were flung into the sea to drown by their wicked mother. If you should be they, restored to me, the dancing apple and the bird which tells the truth will know my wife for the one who would have murdered you.' And he had the young Queen brought from her tower. Pale and in rags she stood before him. 'Let the apple dance,' said the King, 'and let the bird tell the truth.'

The little Prince laid the dancing apple, red as blood, upon the table, and it began to dance. It danced and danced, right across the table, and then it danced right on to the head of the King's stepmother, and then it vanished, never to be seen again.

The widow-Queen cried out in fear, 'It is not true. There she stands, the one who would have murdered your children.' And she pointed at the young Queen.

But the bird of truth spoke shrilly. 'It is the truth, O King. There she sits, your stepmother, who hated your queen and caused your children to be thrown into the sea.' And the bird told the whole story of the widow-Queen's deception, and then it vanished for ever. And the widow-Queen rose up in terror and confessed her guilt, imploring mercy.

'What mercy can there be for you?' said the King. And he turned from her in horror and took his queen in his arms and kissed her, begging her forgiveness for having doubted her. Then they both embraced their children, and never could four people have been happier than they in that hour.

As for the widow-Queen, she was driven away from the castle, never to return, power and pomp lost to her for ever. But the old fisherman and his wife were brought to the castle to live in comfort and plenty for the rest of their lives.

The Miller and the Ogre

A<small>T</small> the foot of a hill there once lived a poor miller with his wife and their seven children: three boys and four girls. All day long the miller worked, grinding wheat into flour for the neighbouring farmers, or growing turnips and cabbages in his little garden; and all day long the miller's wife worked, caring for her children, scrubbing, mending, and racking her wits to think how to cook a tasty meal with very little to put in the pot. Besides his few poor sticks of furniture, there was nothing the miller owned in the world save a few hens and one old black cow. His wife milked the cow, and from the milk she made a little butter to sell in the village. And so they lived from day to day, never sure what tomorrow might bring.

In a castle at the top of the hill lived an ogre with his wife and their servant. This ogre considered himself to own the hill on which his castle stood and all the land that lay around it, and he was pleased to demand rent from the miller for the mill, which he said was his: a tithe of all that was paid for grinding corn, and two large sacks of flour besides. Once a year the ogre would come striding down the hill to collect his dues, and since he was large and bad tempered, what could the miller do but pay? Though it was never easy to find either the money or the flour, with nine hungry mouths to feed.

One year the crops failed and there was little corn to grind, and so less money than usual to buy food, and none at all to pay the ogre. All the flour that the miller had saved, his wife made into bread for the children, and try as they might, they could spare none for the ogre. So it was with great fear that they awaited his visit.

When it drew near the time that the ogre usually came, the miller had his children keep watch in turn to give him warning of the ogre's approach. One evening the miller and his family had just finished their supper—and a simple and scant enough one it had been, too—when the second eldest boy, whose turn it was to keep watch, cried out in a great fright, 'Father, father, the ogre is coming down the hill.' The miller ran to look, and there, sure enough, was the ogre striding down the hill with his club in his hand.

'Quickly, quickly, there is no time to lose,' said the miller as he locked the door of the mill. He hurried his family into the barn where the big heap of straw and chaff stood, and he made them all crawl into it, one after another, while he counted them as they disappeared, wriggling like so many eels: 'One, two, three, four, five, six, seven, eight.' And when he had made sure that not a wisp of hair, not the tip of a sabot, showed, then it was the miller's turn to hide. He burrowed his way into the dusty heap and dragged a large sack over himself; and there they all waited in fear and trembling.

The ogre strode up to the mill door and beat a loud rat-tat on it. When he got no answer, he hammered on the door with his club for a full two minutes. Then he tried the latch and found the door was locked. He roared out threats to the miller and peered in through a window, and then he went off, very angry and shouting that he would be back again. He looked about him as he went, hoping for a sight of at least one of the miller's children, but he saw nobody, nothing save the miller's old black cow, peacefully chewing the cud on the plot of grass before the mill, tethered to a long rope attached to a peg in the ground. The ogre was so angry that, out of sheer spite, he went over to the cow and hit it smartly between the horns with his great club, so that the poor beast fell dead, all in a moment. Then he stamped his way back up the hill to his castle.

As soon as it was safe, the miller and his family crept out from the heap, coughing and sneezing and covered with dust. But at least they were safe from the ogre for another day or two. At first they were inclined to congratulate themselves on the cleverness of the miller's ruse, as they emptied the chaff out of their sabots and picked straws out of each other's clothes and hair; but when they saw what he had done to their cow, then there was such a wailing and such a swearing that they would get even with him from nine loud voices all at once, that they must have all but deafened themselves.

However, all things end, and at last the miller said, 'Come, wife, there is no use in crying over spilt milk. I will skin the old cow and see what I can get for her hide, and you might as well see what can be done with a few joints of beef. The hide may fetch a silver piece or two, and the meat will certainly put a little flesh on our bones.' The miller skinned the cow, and they cut up the meat into joints and filled a bladder with the blood, and then they all went to bed.

The miller was up soon after midnight, and with the cowskin slung over one shoulder, he set off for the market in the nearest town, to make sure of being the first one there with a hide to sell. His way led him by a forest path, and as he plodded along in the darkness, he was aware of several lanterns and of voices approaching him. Fearing robbers, he scrambled up into the branches of a tree beside the path, dragging the cowskin with him, and there he waited quietly, until the strangers should have gone by. But to his great distress, when they came below the tree where he was hidden, they stopped and threw down three or four sacks which they carried, and then by the light of their lanterns they emptied the sacks upon the ground. The miller had been quite right about their being robbers, as he saw at once when the sacks were opened and golden coin after golden coin rolled out and the robbers settled down to divide their gains between them.

The miller was so frightened that he began to tremble. The leaves of the tree rustled and his teeth chattered and the robbers looked up. 'What is that?' cried one of them. Terrified, the miller lost his balance, gave a wild yell, clutched at a branch and dropped his cowskin. The black cowskin with its horns, the tail and all four hoofs flying, fell straight down on to the robbers and their booty. What with the miller's yell and this dreadful monster falling upon them out of the darkness, the robbers leapt up in panic and fled, calling 'Heaven protect us!' believing that it was the devil come to take them to the other place.

When all was quiet, the miller climbed down from the tree and refilled the sacks with the gold, laid them on the cowskin, and dragged it home after him, with the greatest difficulty, for it was very heavy. Exhausted, he arrived home at dawn and roused his wife to come and help him count his treasure. At midday they were still counting and were not half-way done. 'It is a pity we have no bushel measure, we could then weigh out the gold,' said the miller's wife.

'The ogre no doubt has a bushel measure,' said the miller bitterly. 'The ogre has everything, and grudges us our bare living.' Suddenly an idea came into his head, and he and his wife whispered together for the next minute or two. Then the miller's wife put her shawl around her head and walked up the hill to the ogre's castle. She knocked politely on the kitchen door, and the ogre's servant opened to her. 'Could you kindly lend me a bushel measure?' she asked. 'My husband the miller has some gold to weigh, and we have no measure large enough.'

The ogre's servant stared at her, scratching his head in bewilderment. 'A bushel measure to weigh gold?'

At that moment, the ogre's unpleasant wife, hearing voices, poked her sharp nose round the kitchen door. 'What is happening?' she demanded. As soon as she saw the miller's wife, she snapped, 'What do you want? I wonder you have the face to show yourself up here, so much rent you owe my husband. Be off with you!'

The miller's wife dropped her a curtsy. 'We shall not owe it much longer, madam. My husband has had a piece of good fortune. So much gold, madam, you never saw the like of it. I was just asking your man here for the loan of a bushel measure to weigh it in.'

'A bushel measure for gold! You must be out of your mind.'

'Oh, no, madam, I assure you.'

'Nonsense!'

They made so much noise between them that the ogre came stamping into the kitchen, roaring out that they were disturbing him with their chatter. When he saw the miller's wife he glared at her. 'So it is you, is it? Well, you can tell your husband from me that he had better pay his rent by tomorrow, or it will be the worse for him.'

The miller's wife dropped him a curtsy. 'Indeed, sir, he means to. Or today, if you prefer it. He has had a piece of good fortune, and it is all thanks to you. If you had not killed our old cow he would never have taken her hide to the market to sell and he would never have come home with four sacks of gold. Just think of it, sir, so much gold that we cannot count it all, and I am come to borrow a bushel measure to weigh it in.'

The ogre roared at her for fully five minutes, calling her

a liar; but at last he calmed down enough to say, 'I shall go and see for myself.'

So the ogre strode down the hill with the miller's wife trotting beside him to keep up with his huge strides, and at the mill they found the miller surrounded by piles of gold. The ogre stared at it with his mouth wide open. When he could speak, he said, 'Did you really get that for taking one cowskin to market?'

'Certainly I did, sir. Four sacks of gold.'

'Good-day,' said the ogre abruptly, and he was gone. The miller and his family looked at each other and laughed fit to split their sides.

Now, the ogre pastured his herd on the other side of the hill and there were forty fine cows in his herd. All the way up to the castle he was calculating how many sacks of gold he could get for their hides, and he had just reached the figure of one hundred and sixty when he hurried in through his door. He shouted to his servant, 'Go at once, at once, mind you, and kill all my cows, skin them and take the hides to market. You should sell each hide for four sacks of gold. But hurry, for hides are fetching a good price today, and if you are slow, the price may have dropped.'

The ogre's servant did as he was told, but naturally, when he got to market and asked four sacks of gold for each hide, he was laughed at; and when he protested that that was the price being paid for skins, he was called a madman. In the end, he went home with barely forty silver pieces, and it is easy to imagine what sort of a reception he had from his master.

Down in the mill, the miller and his family were waiting for supper. The stew was boiling and bubbling in the pot over the fire, when the eldest girl, whose turn it was to keep watch, called out in a great fright, 'Father, father, the ogre is coming down the hill.'

'Quickly,' said the miller, who had been expecting this. 'Help me to carry the pot outside.'

They carried out the pot of steaming stew and set it on the grass, and the miller took up a whip and hopped around the pot, whipping it. 'Hurry up, pot,' he said, 'we are all hungry.'

The ogre strode up to the mill, swinging his club and calling out for the miller. 'You rogue, you rascal, just you wait till I have got hold of you.' When he saw the miller, he stopped dead. 'What in the world are you doing, miller? Have you gone mad?'

The miller looked surprised to see the ogre there. 'Why indeed no, sir. I am just cooking the stew for supper.'

'Cooking it without a fire, on the grass?' roared the ogre.

'Ah, but you see, sir, this is a magic pot, it cooks food without a fire if you just whip it for a minute or two.'

'Of all the liars!' said the ogre. Then he came nearer and he saw the stew boiling merrily in the pot, for it was still hot from being on the fire, and he smelt the good beef stew and remembered that he had not had his own supper yet. 'I will have your pot,' he said. 'I shall find it most useful.'

'But wood is so dear,' wailed the miller. 'What shall I do without my pot?'

'Eat your food uncooked,' said the ogre. And without waiting for the miller to agree, he took up the pot, stew and all, and carried it up the hill to his castle; while the miller and his family laughed fit to split their sides.

Of course, by the time the ogre had reached the castle, the stew was cold, and no amount of whipping could make it boil again. The ogre's servant sniggered, the ogre's wife told him nastily what a fool he was, the ogre's arm ached from whipping the pot, and he was in a fury. 'You wait,' he shouted, 'tomorrow I shall go down to the mill again, and that miller will be sorry he was ever born.'

Early the next morning, the eldest boy, whose turn it was to keep watch, called out in a great fright, 'Father, father, the ogre is coming down the hill.'

The miller, who had been expecting this sooner or later, took the bladder filled with cow's blood and hung it around his wife's neck, arranging her shawl over it so that it could not be seen. 'Now remember to play your part well, wife,' he said.

'You can trust me, husband,' she promised.

As soon as the ogre's angry roars could be heard outside the mill, the miller and his wife began to rail at one another. 'Shrew! Slut! Idle gossip!' shouted the miller, shaking his fists at his wife. 'Bully! Wine-bibber! Good-for-nothing!' shrieked his wife, threatening him with a wooden ladle.

They made so much noise that even the ogre's roaring was drowned, and he stopped in the doorway, surprised, for he had always believed the miller and his wife to be a peaceable pair, unlike himself and his old scold up at the castle. Suddenly, the miller took up a large knife from the table and drove it into the bladder, so that all the blood streamed out. The miller's wife gave one great scream, fell down on the floor and lay still.

'Villain! Murderer!' exclaimed the ogre. 'First you trick me into killing all my fine cows, all forty of them, and now I catch you killing your wife. It will be the hangman's rope for you, miller, before you can do any more harm.'

'Good morning to you, sir,' said the miller, as though he had only just realized that the ogre was there. 'Never you worry about me and my wife. This often happens. I have a quick temper, you know. But it does her no harm, thanks to my magic bellows.' He went to the fireplace and picked up the bellows. 'See, sir, this is all I have to do.' And he blew gently with the bellows into each of his wife's nostrils, and she sat up on the floor. She threw up her hands as though in horror at seeing the ogre there. 'Oh, sir, what a time to come visiting us, just when my husband has killed me again! Here am I in such a pickle, with my cap all crooked and my apron—clean this morning, too —all covered in blood. Really, husband, you are too provoking.'

The ogre paid no attention to her chatter. He pointed to the bellows which the miller still held. 'I might find those bellows useful. Give them to me.'

'But, sir, what shall I do next time I kill my wife?'

'Bury her,' said the ogre. And without waiting for the miller to agree, he snatched the bellows from him and was away up the hill to his castle; while the miller and his family laughed fit to split their sides.

The ogre's wife met him at the door. 'Well, and have you settled your score with that wretch of a miller?'

'To be sure, I forgot all about it. But here, wife, I have a fine thing. A magic bellows which can bring the dead back to life.'

'Never tell me the miller has tricked you again! Of all the fools in the world, you must be the biggest.' And she was off on one of her speeches. The ogre tried to get a word in edgeways, but it was no use. It never was any use when his wife was nagging. Then he thought, 'This time I will teach her a lesson.' And he pulled out the knife at his belt and cut her throat from ear to ear. He let her stay dead until midday, so that she had time to learn the lesson, and then he began to feel hungry and think about a meal. He took the bellows and blew into her nostrils. He blew and blew until he was crimson in the face from working the bellows, but still she stayed dead—which was not surprising, seeing that he had cut her throat. When at last he realized how he had been tricked, he tore his hair and ran roaring about the castle, for though his wife had been no beauty and her tongue no loss, she had been a very good cook, and his servant, on the other hand, did not know beans from barley.

Down at the mill, the miller had just finished wiping the gravy from his plate with a piece of bread, and was pushing his plate away from him to take up his mug and drink off the last of his wine, at the very moment when the ogre and his servant strode out of the castle. This time it was the turn of the fourth girl, who was the youngest of all the children, to keep watch, and being very young indeed, she was so frightened when she saw both the ogre and his servant coming down the hill, that she gave one little squeak which the miller never heard, and ran to hide in the heap of straw and chaff.

So this time the miller was taken by surprise, which is not really to be wondered at, as one's luck cannot last for ever. The ogre picked him up, dropped him into one of his own flour sacks and watched while his servant fastened the sack tightly with a cord; then he swung the sack up over his shoulder and set off for the river. However, the river was a mile or two away and the day was hot, and only a short distance from the river, beside the road, there was an inn. 'This is thirsty work,' said the ogre, mopping his brow. 'I am going into the inn.' He laid the sack down beside the road. At the door of the inn he turned to his servant and said with unwonted good humour, 'As we are celebrating the end of that rascally miller, I will buy you some wine as well.' The servant grinned delightedly and hurried after his master, and the miller in his sack was left alone by the road.

He struggled and wriggled for all he was worth, but the sack was a strong one and the knots were tied tightly, and it was no use. Just as he had given up hope, he heard the clip clop of little hoofs along the road, and a merchant came by with his wares to sell, laden upon twelve donkeys. 'Let me out, good friend, let me out,' cried the miller.

The merchant stopped and walked around the sack. 'Why should I let you out?

'Because I am in trouble and I need your help.'

The merchant kicked the sack. 'I have enough to do looking after my donkeys and getting my goods to market, without stopping to let strangers out of sacks. Find someone else to help you.' He cracked his whip. 'Get along there!' he shouted to the donkeys.

'Stop, stop!' said the miller. 'You must help me. I am a merchant like yourself. A rich nobleman is carrying me off to his castle. His daughter fancies a merchant for a husband and the wedding is to be today. I am to have the girl and half her father's wealth. But I have a wife already, and besides, I like being poor.'

'The more fool you,' said the merchant. 'You would not find me refusing such an offer.'

'Then take my place,' suggested the miller. 'So long as she marries a merchant, the girl will not mind who he is.'

The merchant thought it over for a moment, while the miller in his sack wrung his hands together and prayed that the ogre would stay in the inn for a second mug of wine. Then the merchant said, 'Out of the sack with you, and I will take your place.' He untied the sack, tipped the miller out on to the dusty road, and stepped into the sack. 'Now you stay here with my donkeys and see that none of them strays. Touch none of my goods. I shall come back this evening, after I have made sure of the girl and the money. If I find that you have taken good care of my property, I may give you the price of a drink from the inn.'

'I will take good care of your property, never fear,' said the miller. And he pulled the sack over the merchant's head and tied it up with the cord. Then he picked up the merchant's whip and cracked it with such good effect that the donkeys broke into a trot, and all twelve of them and the miller himself were just out of sight round the bend of the road when the ogre and his servant came out of the inn.

The ogre picked up the sack, carried it to the river and flung it in. He rubbed his hands together in satisfaction. 'That is the end of the miller at last. We might as well return to the inn.' But he was wrong, for it was the end of the merchant.

The miller arrived at the market, chose a place to display his wares, and unloaded the donkeys. He found that the merchant had traded in trinkets: rings, belts, brooches, buckles, mostly silver-gilt and coloured glass, pretty enough things, which would sell at a fair price. He was doing good trade when he heard a merry catch roared out in the ogre's well-known voice, and he looked up to see the ogre and his servant, arm in arm, strolling between the booths, eying the things for sale. They were both swaying slightly; but while the servant was concentrating on placing one foot carefully before the other without falling down, the ogre was singing heartily, and seemed in a better temper than the miller ever remembered seeing him. For all that, the miller looked about him for somewhere to hide, but before he could find anywhere, the ogre was standing in front of his stall, his mouth wide open. He pointed an accusing finger. 'Miller, you ought to be at the bottom of the river. I put you there myself.'

'To be sure you did, sir, and I owe you my thanks for it. Look what I found at the bottom of the river.' He waved his hand about him. 'All these goods to sell, and twelve donkeys to carry them.'

'You are a lucky fellow and no mistake,' said the ogre. 'Did you bring all the goods with you, or were there any left?'

'There were plenty more,' said the miller, 'and far better than these. Real gold and silver, the other things were. But I thought it would look odd if a poor fellow like myself tried to sell gold and silver in a market.' He lowered his voice. 'They might think I had stolen it, you know, sir.'

'Yes, yes. Very wise of you,' said the ogre. He pulled his servant along, back the way they had come. 'Hurry, hurry, you blockhead. I do believe you are drunk. Hurry, hurry, or someone else will get to the river first.'

At that spot where he had thrown the merchant into the river, the ogre stopped. 'In with you, and tell me what you can see.' And he picked up his servant and flung him into the water. The servant sank, then rose to the surface, gasping and spluttering. He could not swim and he waved wildly at the ogre for help. 'You have seen the gold and silver? Good fellow. Wait for me.' And the ogre leapt far out into the river. But he could not swim either, so neither of them ever got home to the castle on the hill.

The miller, however, got safely home that same evening, with twelve donkeys, a few unsold trinkets which he gave to his wife and daughters, and a fat bag of money which he shared out amongst the three boys. For he could well afford to do so, still having all the robbers' gold to spend.

The Three Oranges

ALONG time ago there was a king who had a daughter as good as she was beautiful. But when she reached the age of eighteen years, she suddenly fell ill of a sickness of which no one could tell the cause. The King sent for all those in his kingdom who knew anything of medicine and healing, and he offered a great sum of gold to anyone who could cure her.

When they had seen the Princess, the learned doctors shook their heads and said, 'We cannot cure her. But far, far away, in the land where the orange-trees grow, there is a garden where the snow never falls. In this garden there is an orange-tree, all covered with white blossom, where seven hundred nightingales sing day and night. From the branches of this tree hang nine oranges. If a man were to fetch her three of these oranges, the Princess would be cured. When she had eaten the first orange she would rise up from her bed. When she had eaten the second she would grow even more beautiful than she is now. And when she had eaten the third orange she would say, "I will marry no one but the man who has brought me the three oranges." '

So the King proclaimed throughout his kingdom that he would give his daughter in marriage to the man who brought her three oranges from the garden in the far-off land.

Now, in that country, at that time, a poor widow lived with her three sons in a tumbledown cottage. The two elder sons were lazy and shiftless and good-for-nothing; but the youngest son was a cheerful, kindly lad who worked hard enough for three, and was, besides, always ready to help anyone who needed help.

When the eldest son heard the proclamation of the King, he said to his mother, 'Give me a basket and food for a journey. I am going to the land where the orange-trees grow. It would be a pleasant thing to marry the Princess and live in ease all my life.'

His mother gave him a basket and food, and off he went. For seven weeks he walked from dawn to darkness, and at last he came to the land where the orange-trees grow. And there he found the garden where it never snowed. In this garden stood the orange-tree, all covered with white blossom, where seven hundred nightingales sang day and night. From the branches of the tree hung nine oranges. The eldest brother plucked three of them, put them into his basket, and set off for home.

For seven weeks he walked from dawn to darkness, and when he was only a mile or two from the palace of the

King, well pleased with himself, he sat down to rest beneath a tree. As he sat there he saw an old woman come by. She stopped and looked at his basket. 'Young man,' she said, 'what have you in that basket?'

'What concern is that of yours, old fool?' thought the eldest brother. And he frowned and said, 'I have three frogs in that basket.'

'Three frogs,' repeated the old woman. 'So be it.' And she went on her way.

That evening the eldest brother arrived at the castle of the King. Being brought before the King, he said, 'I have here three oranges, and I claim the hand of your daughter.'

Eagerly the King opened the basket and out jumped three frogs, croaking loudly. And in great anger the King called for the hangman to hang the eldest brother.

When fourteen weeks had passed and the eldest brother had not returned home, the second brother said to his mother, 'Give me a basket and food for a journey. I am going to the land where the orange-trees grow. I have a fancy to marry the Princess and be a rich man all my life.'

His mother gave him a basket and food, and off he went. For seven weeks he walked from dawn to darkness, and at last he came to the land where the orange-trees grow. And there in the garden where snow never fell, from the tree covered with white blossom where seven hundred night-ingales sang day and night, he plucked three oranges and put them in his basket. Then he set off for his own land once again.

When he was but a mile or two from the palace of the King, he sat down to rest beneath the very same tree where

his brother had rested, and while he sat there he saw an old woman come by. 'Young man,' she said, 'what have you in that basket?'

'What concern is that of yours, old hag?' thought the second brother. And he scowled and said, 'Three snakes.'

'Three snakes,' repeated the old woman. 'So be it.' And she went on her way.

That evening the second brother arrived at the castle of the King, and being brought before him, he said, 'I have here three oranges, and I claim the hand of your daughter.'

Eagerly the King opened the basket, and out crawled three hissing snakes. And in great anger the King called for the hangman to hang the second brother.

When another fourteen weeks had passed and neither of his brothers had come home, the youngest brother said to his mother, 'Dear mother, give me a basket and food for a journey. With your blessing I am going to the land where the orange-trees grow. If I can cure the Princess, I may earn a little money for you.'

His mother gave him a basket and food and her blessing, and off he went. For seven weeks he walked from dawn to darkness, and at last he came to the land where the orange-trees grow. And there from the tree in the garden he plucked the last three oranges and put them in his basket. Then he set off for his own land once again.

When he was but a mile or two from the palace he sat down to rest beneath the very same tree where his brothers had rested. And while he sat there, the old woman came by. 'Young man,' she said, 'what have you in that basket?'

The youngest brother smiled at her. 'Three oranges, good grandmother.'

'Three oranges,' she repeated. 'So be it. And what will you do with three oranges, my friend?'

'I am taking them to the castle of the King, that his daughter may be cured of her sickness. He has promised her hand to the man who brings her the three oranges, but I am only a peasant, I am too poor to marry a princess. Yet the King may reward me with a little money which I can give to my mother.'

'My friend,' said the old woman, 'you shall marry the Princess. But before that comes to pass, the King will ask you to perform three tasks. If you will take the gifts I give you, the tasks will not be hard.' And she took out from under her cloak a whip, a silver whistle, and a golden ring. 'With this whip one can chase away flies, with this whistle one can call together hares, and when this ring is placed on the finger of the Princess, it will fit so tightly that she will cry out to the King, "I shall die if you do not allow me to marry the man who has brought me the three oranges." '

The youngest brother took the three gifts, thanked the old woman, and went on to the castle of the King. When he came there and stood before the King, he said, 'Your majesty, I have here three oranges for your daughter.'

Eagerly the King opened the basket and saw the oranges, bright as gold. 'Here are indeed three oranges,' he said, well pleased.

When the Princess had eaten the first orange, she rose up from her bed. When she had eaten the second, she became even more beautiful than she had been before. And when she had eaten the third orange, she said, 'I will marry no one but the man who has brought me the three oranges.'

But the King looked askance at the youngest brother and thought, 'He is only a peasant lad, why should my daughter wed with such as he?' And he said, 'You shall marry my daughter if you can drive all the flies from my kingdom, for ever.'

'It shall be done, your majesty,' said the youngest brother. And he cracked the whip which the old woman had given him, and at the sound all the flies in the kingdom flew far, far away, never to return.

But the King looked askance at the youngest brother and said, 'I will give you my daughter if you can gather together all the hares in my kingdom and bring them to my stables.'

'It shall be done, your majesty,' said the youngest

brother. And he went out into the fields and he blew on the silver whistle, and instantly, from everywhere, hares came bounding towards him. When he had gathered them together, all three hundred of them, he returned to the castle, blowing on his whistle, and the hares followed him as though they had been dogs.

'I have done as you commanded, your majesty.'

But still the King looked askance at him. 'Out of those three hundred hares, catch for me the one I want,' he said.

'It shall be done, your majesty. But permit me first to put this ring upon the finger of your daughter.'

'As you will,' replied the King, seeing no harm in the request.

The youngest brother put the golden ring on the finger of the Princess, and at once, as the old woman had said, it became so tight that she cried out, 'Father, I shall die if you do not allow me to marry the man who brought me the three oranges.'

The King knew that he could no longer refuse the reward that he had promised. 'You shall marry him tomorrow, my child,' he said. And immediately the ring fitted her finger perfectly, as though it had been made for her.

And so the youngest brother married the Princess, and they lived happily for many, many years. And he gave his mother money and a fine house besides, and she worked no more for the rest of her days.

The Mouse-Princess

IN the days that are passed there lived a king who had
three sons. He had ruled well and wisely for more years
than he liked to remember, and one day he thought to
himself how he was growing old and might well hand the
cares of state and governing to a younger man, so that for
the time that remained to him he might enjoy a well-
earned rest, while one of his sons took his place as king.
But the problem that faced him was to which of his three
sons he should give his crown and the responsibility that
went with it.

The two elder princes were gay, gallant young men, at
home in any company and well liked by everyone; but the
youngest was a quiet, shy youth, well meaning and kindly
enough, but given too much to thinking and reading to
meet with his brothers' approval, and, let it be said, over
fond of his own company to be altogether pleasing to
others. The King saw the merits of each of his sons, but he

205

saw also their disabilities. The two elder were perhaps a little too casual and easy going, a degree too fond of letting things look after themselves; while the youngest was, it is undeniable, rather too serious-minded, and given, besides, to making mountains out of mole-hills.

As the King was pondering his problem, he remembered the young men's mother, his good queen who was dead, and he thought, 'Whatever a man is, it is his wife who helps him to be what he will become. Whichever of my sons succeeds me, if he has a good queen, he will be half-way to being a good king.' He considered then the qualities which go to make a good queen, having always in his mind the picture of his own beloved wife. 'She must be patient,' he thought, 'she must be neat and deft, and she must not despise the simple, necessary things of life. Yet she must have beauty and dignity and noble bearing, and above all, she must be gracious and truly royal.'

The King sent for his three sons, and to each of them he handed a hank of flax, saying, 'I would know what manner of maiden she is who may one day be queen in your dear mother's place. Go, each of you, and give this flax to the lady of your choice, bid her spin it into thread, and when seven days are passed, bring me the thread she has spun.'

The two elder brothers each loved a noble maiden of the court, the one a countess and the other the daughter of a duke, and at once they took the flax and went to their ladies, repeating their father's words and saying that they doubted not that on the results of their spinning would rest the choice of a successor. The Countess and the Duke's daughter were both proud and beautiful; indeed, there was little to choose between them for looks and arrogance. They were skilled in all the accomplishments of noble-women: they could sing prettily enough and play upon the lute, and they could dance a measure trippingly; but they had never learnt to spin. However, when she saw a crown within her grasp, each of them eagerly set to work upon the flax, bidding her lover have no fear of the result.

But the youngest brother had no lady whom he loved. He was shy and confused in the company of maidens, feel-ing that they despised him for his lack of gallantry and his inability to talk sweet nonsense which he did not mean. He took his hank of flax, put it in his pocket, and rode out alone from the palace into the forest, depressed and despon-dent, worrying and teasing himself as to what his father would say to him, in seven days' time, when he gave him back the unspun flax. But he knew that he could not, not even to gain a crown, ask any maiden to spin the flax for him, and risk her scorn and her refusal.

Now, in a neighbouring kingdom, a few years before, the daughter of the King and Queen had had the misfortune to displease a witch, who had immediately turned her into a mouse. 'A mouse shall you stay,' the witch had said, 'until you have made me laugh.' As that witch had never been known to laugh, and was, besides, very ill-tempered, there seemed no likelihood of the Princess ever regaining her own shape. The King and the Queen would have been ready to care for their daughter in the form of a mouse for the rest of their lives, and give her every comfort: the best cheese for every meal and a room with ample holes in the wainscotting; but there were too many cats in that palace, and the mouse-princess took fright and ran away, right out of the palace and right out of the kingdom, and into the land ruled over by the old King who had three sons. There in a forest she came upon a ruined tower, all overgrown with ivy and yellow toadflax, and in this tower she made her home.

On the day when the King had given his sons the flax, the mouse was sitting on top of her ruined wall at the time when the youngest Prince rode by. She saw him come, and kept very still. It was a part of the forest where the Prince had never been before, and when he noticed the ruined tower, he felt that it was well fitted to his mood, and he dismounted and sat down upon a fallen block of stone. Seeing him so dejected, the mouse ran down the wall and went to him. Sitting up on her hind legs a yard or so from his feet, she asked him what ailed him. Had he been a less thoughtful person, he might have been surprised to hear a mouse speak, but as it was, he saw no reason why a mouse should not speak as well as a man. Since a courteous question deserves a courteous reply, the Prince told the mouse his troubles, and when he had finished, she said, 'If you will permit it, I can help you.'

'How can a mouse help me?' asked the Prince.

'Give me the flax and return here in seven days, and you shall see what you shall see.'

Since the Prince had no one else to whom he dared give the flax, he saw no harm in giving it to the mouse. He pulled it out of his pocket, laid it down beside her, thanked her politely and rode away.

Seven days later he returned to the ruined tower, and

there he found the mouse waiting for him, a little box beside her. 'Take this box to the King,' she said, 'and let him open it.'

Being himself kindly and good natured, the Prince did not doubt that the mouse would have done her best for him, and seeing that there was no one else to do as much, he thanked her gratefully and rode back to the palace. When he arrived, he found that his brothers were there before him, bringing the thread spun by their ladies. They laughed at their brother when they saw how he carried no thread but only a little box, and with confidence they gave their spools of thread to the King. He looked at them, turned them this way and that, unwound a length of thread from each, and then he sighed and laid them by. For the Countess's thread was as thick as hempen rope, while the thread spun by the Duke's daughter was so thin and uneven that a child could easily have snapped it. The King smiled encouragingly at his youngest son, who had held back, abashed by his brothers' taunts. 'Where is your thread, my son?' The youngest Prince came forward and held out the little box. 'It is here, father.'

The King took the box and opened it. Inside was a ball of thread as fine as hair and as bright, but so strong that however hard he tugged at it, it would not break.

The two elder brothers looked at one another, eyebrows raised, and the King looked at his youngest son, wondering. But he said nothing, and only laid the ball of thread aside, as he had done with the spools. Then he smiled at his three sons. 'The thread is only the beginning,' he said, 'it is the finished cloth which completes the task.' And he gave to each of the young men a reel of linen thread spun by the chief spinning maid of the palace. It was neither so thick as the Countess's thread, nor yet so fine as the thread which the mouse had given the youngest Prince, and unlike the thread of the Duke's daughter, it was strong enough. 'Go,' he said, 'and give this thread to the ladies of your choice, and bid them weave a length of cloth from it. When seven days are passed, bring the cloth to me.'

The two elder brothers hurried to their ladies, who had, naturally, never learnt to weave. But nothing daunted, thinking of the crown that was so close, they set to work as best they might.

The youngest brother put the reel of thread in his pocket and rode from the palace alone. This time he went straight to the ruined tower in the forest. 'Little mouse, little mouse,' he called, and there she was, her bright eyes gleaming, looking down at him from the top of the wall. 'Did you give the box to the king?' she asked.

'I did, little mouse.'

'And what did he say?'

'Why, he said nothing.'

'That is well,' she replied, and ran down the wall to his feet. 'But why are you still sad?' He told her. 'If you wish it, I will help you,' she said.

He smiled, a little cheered. 'If you would help me again, I should always be grateful.'

'Give me the thread.' He took it out of his pocket and laid it before her. 'Come back in seven days,' she said, 'and you shall see what you shall see.' And he thanked her and rode away.

Seven days later he returned to the ruined tower, and there was the mouse waiting for him, a little box by her side. 'Take this box to the King,' she said, 'and let him open it.'

He spent an hour or two with her, sitting on a block of fallen stone, talking of this and that; and she seemed to him an intelligent and likeable companion indeed. Then he took the little box, thanked her, and rode back to the palace. When he arrived he found his two brothers there before him, bringing the cloth woven by their ladies, and when they saw that he carried nothing but a wooden box which seemed too small to hold a length of cloth, they smiled their relief at each other. With confidence they gave their cloth to the King, who took each length in his hands and sighed and laid it by. The cloth woven by the Countess was so coarse and stiff that it could almost have stood up by itself, while the cloth woven by the Duke's daughter would have made a passable fisherman's net. The King looked at his youngest son. 'Where is your cloth?' he asked.

The youngest Prince held out the little box. 'It is here, father.'

The King opened the box and pulled out, yard by yard, a length of cloth so soft and fine that the small box could easily contain it. Yet it was strong, with the warp and the woof even and smooth.

The two elder brothers looked at one another, frowning and angry, and the King looked at his youngest son, wondering. But he said nothing and only laid the length of cloth aside, next to the others. Then he smiled at his sons.

'I have seen,' he said, 'what your ladies can do, and how skilled they are. But surely the final test of fitness to be a queen is in the bearing of the lady herself, and not in the skill of her hands. At midday tomorrow, let each of you come here with his bride, and I will tell you which of you shall be king in my place.'

The two elder brothers hurried off to the Countess and the Duke's daughter, and the two ladies were thrown into a great flutter. The rest of that day they spent trying on their best gowns, choosing out their finest jewels, and strutting and preening themselves before their mirrors.

But the youngest Prince rode out of the palace, and because it was a habit with him by now, he went to the ruined tower. 'Little mouse, little mouse, are you there?' And there she was, peeping out through a spray of honeysuckle which hung over a window-sill. 'Did you give the box to the King?'

'I did, little mouse.'

'And what did he say?'

'Why, nothing.'

'That is well,' she said. And she ran down the stem of the honeysuckle, out of the window and across to his feet.

'No,' said the Prince, 'it is not well. I shall never be a king.' He sat down upon the grass and the mouse stood beside his hand. 'What has your father asked of you now?' she said.

'That at midday tomorrow I shall bring him the lady who is to be my bride, the lady who spun the thread and wove the cloth. But alas, little mouse, there is no lady.'

The mouse was silent; and the Prince, too, said nothing

for many minutes, then he looked at the mouse and saw a large tear trickling down her nose. He tried hard to smile and to sound as though he did not care. 'This time you cannot help me, little mouse, but you have done enough already, and you must not think that I am ungrateful because I am sad.' He took a ring off his finger. 'See, here is a gift for you to remember me by.' He laid it gently beside her on the grass and stood up. 'Good-bye, little mouse, and thank you.' He mounted his horse and rode away, and she cried out after him, 'I will help you. I will find a way.' But he only turned and shook his head and smiled at her.

All that night the mouse-princess thought and thought, but she could think of no way to help the Prince, and in the morning she still had no plan. But as it approached mid-day, she could not bear not to be with him to comfort him when his brothers came with their brides and he had none. So she picked up his ring in her mouth and she ran and she ran through the forest until she reached the highway. And there she stopped, for she could run no farther. At that moment a man came by with a crate of chickens for the market. The mouse stepped out into his path, dropped the ring, sat up and spoke to him. 'Good friend,' she said, 'give me your black cock, and make me a bridle and saddle, that I may ride on him.'

The man was so surprised to hear a mouse speak and so amused by her request, that he thought, 'It will be worth the loss of the price of my black cock, just to have such a story to tell.' He made a bridle out of plaited grasses and a saddle out of a dock leaf, and saddled and bridled the cock. The mouse thanked him, took up the ring in her mouth and mounted upon the back of the cock, and away they went, towards the palace of the King.

Now, it happened that the way to the palace lay past the castle where the witch lived who had put the spell on the

Princess, and her servant was at the window when the mouse rode by on the cock. The servant burst out laughing. 'Idle wench,' scolded the witch, 'what are you laughing at?'

'Why, mistress, I have never seen such a sight in my life!' But the girl could say no more for laughing.

'You foolish creature,' said the witch, and she came angrily to the window. But when she looked out and saw the mouse riding on the cock, she, who had never been known even to smile, found herself laughing until the tears ran down her cheeks. And in that moment the mouse became a princess, in silk and velvet and pearls, with a crown upon her head, riding on a black horse with green and golden trappings.

Promptly at midday, the two elder Princes, with their brides beside them, came before the King; and the youngest Prince followed after them, alone.

Nothing could have been more splendid than the sight offered by the Countess and the Duke's daughter. Their gowns were so stiff with jewels that it was a marvel the ladies could move at all, and they flashed so brightly that the King's eyes were almost dazzled. And as for their regal dignity, why, if the Countess had tilted her head much higher, she would surely have tripped and fallen; while as for the disdain of the Duke's daughter, it seemed to include even the King himself.

The two elder brothers presented their brides, and the two ladies curtsied to the King. He spoke to them kindly, and kissed each of them upon the cheek. 'You have my blessing, daughters,' he said. He turned to the two Princes. 'My sons, you have chosen suitably.' The Princes bowed to their father and kissed his hand, self-satisfaction glowing in their hearts, for they had not seen the twinkle in his eyes. But the Countess and the Duke's daughter glared haughtily at one another over their bridegrooms' heads, all their past friendship forgotten in their present rivalry.

The King beckoned to his youngest son. 'Where is your bride?' he asked.

The youngest Prince knelt before his father. 'Father, I have none,' he said, and hung his head in shame, whilst his brothers grinned at one another.

At that moment the chamberlain hurried in and whispered to the King. The King smiled a little. 'Bring her in,' he said.

A minute or so later, the Princess was curtseying to the King, and a few seconds after that, she was standing by the youngest Prince; and there was not a lady in all that court who would not have seemed like a serving-wench beside her.

'Look up, my son,' said the King, 'and see your bride.'

The Prince looked up and saw the loveliest maiden he had ever dreamt of, with a crown upon her head; unconscious of the richness of her garments, graceful and gracious and perfectly at ease, she smiled at him, and he felt neither awkward nor shy. He rose and asked in wonder, 'Who are you?'

'I am your bride,' she said.

He looked at her and loved her in that instant; then he looked at his brothers and saw their anger, he looked at the Countess and at the Duke's daughter and saw their jealousy and of how little worth they were, and he looked at the King and saw the smile on his lips, and he knew that he had but to say a single word and the crown would be his. Yet he could not say that word. He turned away from the Princess and said, 'This is not my bride. If any should be my bride, it should be the little mouse who spun the yarn and wove the cloth for me.'

'But I was the mouse,' said the Princess. 'See, here is your ring.' And she held it out to him. He took it and put it on her finger and kissed her; and that is the end of the tale.